AF243684

# ORBIT BEACH

## JANE ETARIE

MURDER ISLAND PRESS

A Golden Hebrew Book
Published by Murder Island Press
Cover Art by Dude Esquire Design
Book Design by Mu Maison

ISBN-13: 978-0-9880515-1-5
ISBN-10:      0-9880515-1-6



www.janeetarie.com

Tom, J, Dave: Thanks.

# ORBIT BEACH

# ONE

# Lost

GLEN GREEN IS A PEAR

Oh my god, not again. I didn't know what the hell it meant the first time I saw it, and I still didn't know what the hell it meant like the fourth time I saw it. I guess it meant I was lost. I guess it meant I was a retard. I guess it meant I was going around in circles like that big shit that wouldn't go down the toilet this morning. That's what the hell it meant.

I mean, it was kind of funny at first. Like a big joke. Like where the fuck's my car? Look at me, I'm so fucking stupid I forgot where I parked. But after a few laps, I was all like, this is not cute, this is so not cute. How could this be happening to me? Why me? I just wanted to cry. I just wanted to get home. I was tired and cranky, my feet hurt, I was getting hungry, and I was out of vodka. So I started panicking. Seriously, I was terrified. Like I couldn't breathe. I was all like, Where is my car? Where is my car? Oh please god help me find my car.

So I guess I prayed? I was like, Please god... I'll be a better person... I'll do anything you want. I'll lose ten pounds. I'll lose twenty pounds. Just please help me find my car. I'll help lost children or something. I don't know. I'll be nicer to bums and old people and the cripples or whatever. I was desperate.

I'd heard when I was younger, like in Brownie Scouts or some shit, that when you are lost, you should stay where you are. So that's what I did. I just sat down on the curb and went into my handbag, half hoping it would somehow show me where my car was. Nope. Nothing there. Keys. Tampons. All sorts of shit to put on my face. Empty mickey. Empty pack of cigarettes, which I threw on the ground. All useless.

I started to cry. I didn't know what I was going to do. I felt helpless. Like I didn't know what I could do or was supposed to do. I'm not sure how long I sat and cried. I found some toilet paper in my handbag. I grabbed a square, pulled apart the plies, and ripped them into strips. One by one they melted in my mouth, and I started to calm down.

I had to admit it—I needed help. I mean, I don't know quit. I don't. But my car was obviously not there. I looked everywhere in that fucking parkade and it definitely was not there. But this totally wasn't my fault. My car got stolen is what happened. I was convinced. I was the innocent victim in all of this. I felt like I'd just been raped.

Some asshole was driving around in my car like a fucking hotshot, laughing and high fiving his criminal friends. Picking up slutty bitches. Picking up nasty hookers. Doing drugs. Listening to *my* gangster rap. Listening to *my* digital music player. Spilling beer. Smoking and cumming all over the interior.

And when those bastards were done their ghetto orgy they'd just strangle the hooker. They'd strangle her and steal her drugs. Snatch the money from her bra. From her thong and her purse. And then they'd shove her in the trunk, with her neck all twisted. Dead. And burn my poor car in some gross hooker alley. In some gross hooker parking lot.

So I called the police. The lady was all like, Nine one one, please state your name and location and some other shit. And I make my voice like it's all cracking, like I have snot coming out of my nose, like I'm trying my best not to cry, like I'm calling in sick to work. And I tell her that I need help, that my car's like stolen, that I'm standing by a pillar that says Glen Green is a Pear at the parkade in the Skycenter Mall. But I'm not so sure where.

And she asks if somebody carjacked me or some shit. Did I see someone steal it? Am I in any physical danger? And I'm like, No. And then she's all like rude and cuts me off and tells me that 911 is for emergencies. That she would connect me to the police department dispatch or whatever.

So after a few minutes some other bitch answers the phone and asks me what my problem is. I tell her what happened, and she starts harassing me with all sorts of stupid questions about my car. She asks if it was stolen in the last twelve hours? Yes. From the location that I was currently at? Yes. Did I call the towing company? Yes I did—but really I didn't. The make, model and year? It was a black 1995 Escalade four wheel drive SUV. And I assure her that even though it's like sixteen years old, it's in great shape. Old lady driven before I bought it. Classic, I tell her, not old. And I don't mention the busted out headlight or the huge ass dent in the rear, in case maybe the insurance will pay for it.

And there is no way I know the VIN or the plate number. There's VG, though, which I remember, because like vag. There's a bumper sticker that says *My Marine Son Protects Your Honor Student*, which was not mine, but I kept on there so the cops wouldn't pull me over after the bar. There's another bumper sticker that says *Bad Girls Drive Bad Toys*. That one was mine. And a decal that says *Bad Girls Drive Bad Toys* on top of the windshield.

I ask her if she can like send an officer or something. That if I could get a ride home that'd be great. And she explains that they can't. That the officers are needed for emergencies, but that she could arrange for a cab if I needed one. And she tells me that if I could get more information and make it in to the detachment later, that I could complete some forms or some shit. But I was done. I just wanted to go home and drink. And I don't think she really cared anyways. Just totally unsympathetic. I felt like she hated me, like she was judging me. Like maybe I'd brought this all on myself, like those raped girls who dress all slutty. I don't know. It was like she secretly enjoyed my misfortune. Enjoyed her job too much. Like she'd been fingering her dirty pig hole the entire time.

Whatever. I wanted to call her a cunt, call her a sick perv and hang up. But sometimes I'm just way too polite. So I was like, All right, thanks... Ok, Sweetie, ok, bye... You have a good night too... ok, bye.

So I'm like all sick and emotional and check my messages while I'm waiting for the cab. And then I get a real kick to the gunt.

Messages:
Boo
i'm br8ing up with u. sorry.

# Change

I think the driver was like Eastern European, like some Russian Polack or some shit. I couldn't understand what the hell he was trying to say, but I think he was trying to be funny, or cheer me up. Like he knew I was upset. He'd look over his shoulder and say something, and then like pause and raise his unibrow, like he's waiting for me to laugh, and then he'd say something else and start laughing. I don't know. I just looked out the dirty window. I wasn't in the fucking mood for his ESL comedy routine.

We got to my place and I realized I didn't have any money on me. I had my bank card, but his cab was old and shitty. So I tell him, like real slow and loud so he can understand, Can you wait a minute? I need to run up to my apartment. I need to go to my apartment to grab some money.

And I don't know what the hell he was saying, like he didn't trust me or like he didn't understand English, but it was like he kept repeating twelve dollar or some shit. You need to give me twelve dollar. Twelve dollar. Twelve dollar. He was starting to sound like that Chocula puppet or whatever. His hairy finger kept tapping his palm, and his unibrow started pointing down.

And it's like, normally I am the most patient person in the world. For serious, I am so patient and understanding that I can easily be taken advantage of. But I was just really upset. I mean, I know he was just trying to do his job, but I didn't care. I didn't care that he came to this country for a better life. From some shit hole that didn't exist anymore. Probably blown up by the Russian army, the women sold into prostitution. And I didn't care that his family had been killed and raped and eaten while he watched. That he had to live like a rat in some gutter of a bombed out building. That he had to live by his wits, like some wild animal, running with the dogs in the streets—his new family—in a country where dog is a source of protein.

I didn't care about any of that. I was just too stressed. Too upset. I was crying. I dug into my jacket pockets. There was a bit of change. There was a lot more change in my purse. Only I was having trouble counting it all over his nagging—What, you call cab and no have twelve dollar? Why you call cab if no twelve dollar? And he was all like going on about how I wasn't going to trick him, how I couldn't trick him. Calling me girl.

It was impossible for me to count the change. I didn't have enough anyways. So I got out the back and came around to his door and was all like, Fuck You! I don't need this shit, you asshole! You fucking terrorist! I was crying, he was so mean. And I grabbed the change I had, I think it was like just over three bucks, and I was all like, Here... here's your fucking money! Take it all!

I admit it—I was hysterical. I threw the dirty pennies and nickels and dimes and some gum wrappers into his cab, so it like went all over the place. He turned and started picking it up like some fucking bum. Like some Transylvanian gypsy bum.

Here... It's all there... Count it. Count it! Go buy yourself some fucking English lessons... buy yourself a ticket back to Russia, you... you fucking Polack...

And I was like bawling and I ran up to my apartment entrance and let myself in. He was still parked out there, penny picking, but I didn't give a shit. He could wait out there all night. I wasn't going to fucking buzz him in.

## Butter

I was so hungry I could've stuffed my face like those fat fuckers on tv. You know, the eleven hundred pound animal who gets his bed forklifted onto the back of a flat deck. Gets paraded around town when he drops a few pounds. Like the dude who has six buckets of greasy chicken smuggled up to his room on a string when his family stops filling the trough. Or the man who gives birth every day to shits the size of two babies, or maybe a couple of big hams.

I keep a picture of one of those beasts on my fridge. And I looked it, and I thought about those sick pigs, and the people who loved them. And it's like, when you love someone enough to remove their two-baby-shit and stink from their room, and wipe their big bedsore ass with some filthy old beach towel—that is true love. That's like real love. Like real devotion. And it made me cry even more.

I checked the fridge. And then I checked the freezer. I needed ice cream. Like those girls on tv, like Jennifer Aniston or some shit, in her T-shirt pyjamas and socks. Like the girls who eat it straight from the tub when they get dumped or when they're on the rag. The entire tub, like they don't even care, like they're crazy. Only I didn't have any ice cream. I didn't have anything. I was left with nothing in this world.

My fridge and cupboards were empty. I'd just finished off a two week cleanse with a food and booze binge. And I never did get to the Whole Foods and Liquor Heaven to restock because I was looking all over the fucking place for my SUV. There were some condiments. Uncle Noberto's Hot Organic Salsa. Real Dijon mustard from Dijon. And some cleanse shit. Chlorophyll, aloe vera, alkaline water, pHour Salts.

And there was no way I was eating the soy butter or tahini. The thought of that tar—that shit—in my mouth, caught in my raw crying throat, choking me, while I struggled to swallow, was too stressful. So I ate an old jar of maraschino cherries before I decided on the tub of butter. I didn't have ice cream, but in my self-loathing and self-pity, butter would do.

I stripped down to my underwear and went to the freezer. I grabbed the Grey Goose and couple mini Jägers and polished them off. I had half a bottle of Syrah that I'd used for cooking and drank that too. And before I hit the Scope, I remembered the bottle of Jamaican rum in the bottom of my closet that a coworker brought me back from her trip.

So I sat in the kitchen, crying, eating my butter, drinking my rum. The butter was actually pretty good. It was like low sodium and whipped. Like artisanal butter. Churned by people in traditional Dutch garments, so it wasn't as gross as you'd think. I had a lot of rum left, but I was worried about running out. And then I had like this flash, like I just remembered something important. My heart raced—I thought I might have some Patrón in the cupboard. Only really I'd drank it a couple of months before. So I got up all clumsy and excited, like some thirty year old retard running down the stairs in his pyjamas on Christmas morning, and I knocked over the butter.

I looked at it on the ground. It didn't even spin on its rim or bounce or move. Just an instant thud, butter side down, like shit. Like dead butter shit. And I felt like everything in the whole world and the whole universe was against me. Like I was a dog being kicked while it was down. Like I'd never catch a break. Like nothing would ever go right for me again. Whatever. I just scraped it off the floor and ate it—I didn't fucking care about anything. But I mean, really, in hindsight, I should have just ordered pizza.

So I called Robert and of course he wasn't picking up his phone. At first I left a few texts, shit like: robert, seriously, we need to talk, please call me. call me asap, ok?... robert what's wrong? we need to talk—call me... robert, let me know what's up, ok?

I was texting and leaving all sorts of messages. I left him like fifty messages. I yelled at him. I cried. Sometimes it was just the sound of me sucking on the bottle. And I don't know why, but in one I was like laughing and talking in an English accent.

And then I was all like, what the hell am I doing? Why am I licking his asshole? He probably loves that I'm grovelling. Loves that I'm begging. Like, What did I do wrong!? What did I do wrong!? Oh please take me back! Having a good laugh that I was sending these pathetic psychotic messages. So I was all like fuck that, the pity party's over.

And I was like seriously thinking about dumping his

sorry ass. Like just forget him and move on. I mean, it's not as if I'm a woman with no prospects. Only I'm the kind of girl who when I love, I love hard, and I love for real. Like I believe that when you're ready for love, and you meet the right person, the Law of Attraction takes over, and love finds you. And the more I thought about it and the more I drank, the more I realized that me and Boo were meant to be together. It's like everyone says, when it's right, you know it's right. When it's the One, you just know it's the One. This was it. He was it. The One. We were like a romance movie. An epic eighties love song. Like one of those books with Fabio on the cover. It's like when Beyoncé sang *Crazy In Love*, she was singing about us. And like when we had sex, it was like that dude in Kings of Leon was singing *Sex is On Fire* just about us. We were like, one of those great loves.

When I was a little girl, I wondered who I'd marry when I grew up. It was like usually a faery tale prince, or Alan Thicke, or my dad or stepdad or something. And when I was about to graduate high school—before I got kicked out for some shit that I didn't even do and wasn't even my fault—I would daydream of what my life would be like. And I know it sounds crazy, but I would wonder like, where is my husband? Where is he right now? Do I already know him? Is he that twenty-five year old guy? That guy parked outside my high school in the flat black Camaro with Slayer painted on the hood? Or maybe he was someone else? What was he doing right now?

And I would come up with all these fantasies. Sometimes he was in prison. All sweaty, pumping iron in the yard. Sent there for like a crime of passion. Or maybe for killing some asshole in self-defense or whatever. He'd be let out soon. We would meet in some shitty bar, and the chemistry would be instant. He'd have crazy ideas, all sorts of crazy ideas, and I would laugh. Like dreams of a better life for us. Like starting up his own custom motorbike shop, or maybe a bar, or a taco stand or whatever. And he'd go out of state to secure a loan with a business partner. Like a prison contact—maybe even a very close cellmate. And then he'd get arrested for breach of parole. And I would wait. I would wait for him and I'd write every day. And he would see our child for the first time when he got out five years later.

Or when I looked at that poster in my locker, he was a Chippendales dancer. A real slut. The third guy on the left with the long blond hair and the killer smile and the killer tan. The tight pants and bow tie. We'd meet at a show. It would be like a bachelorette party for one of my friends. All the bitches are horny and lathered. And he picks me. Out of all my friends, he picks *my* face to swivel his crotch in front of. And after a lap dance and a thong to the face, I'd develop an eye infection. But it's ok, we'd hook up. Because he's like concerned, like sweet, like he wants to take care of me. And we'd have a steamy courtship, and then he'd have to decide—Jet-setting and living high on the hog with the Chippendales, or settling down with me. Only it would be a happy ending—I'd travel with him and watch all the shows with our babies.

And other times he was like a gigolo. A male prostitute. Standing on the corner in his cutoffs, wifebeater, and Doc Martins. With his peach fuzz moustache. So hot. Leaning into old men's cars. Leaning into my car. And he'd kind of mumble when he talked, and always look away, never look you in the eye. Wanna date? Ya. Ya I do. And he would smell like Jean Paul Gaultier's Le Male and I would be his forever.

But as it turned out, that boy—my future husband—was in second grade. And was like about to spend another year in second grade because he was in the hospital for a few months with viral meningitis or some shit.

So I made up my mind. You don't just let something like this slip through your fingers. You don't just let some random bullshit destroy your dream. And I wasn't just going to like throw away the last five months of my life. Five of the best months of my life. Fuck that. I had too much invested in this. And I was done with the dating bullshit. Done. It's like, we only have so much time in this life and I wasn't going to waste any more of it. That window—my time, my youth, my opportunity—was closing fast. My mind was set. My path, my direction, my future was set. I was going to like call Robert back and say, Robert—I am not giving up on you. I am not giving up on our love. You do not just give up on a love like this.

So I phoned him back, but his messages were full. Not bad, universe, not bad. So I texted him. I left him and the universe and the whole shitty world a message. The ace up my sleeve. A sucker punch. A knockout punch. That fucking bomb that killed all those Japanese or Vietnamese or whatever and left that little girl running naked and crying in the street. I felt like what that retard must have felt like after he let everyone know that Glen Green was a pear.


Robert. Please call me. I'm pregnant.

# Morning Sickness

I called in sick this morning. I work at Petrus Cheong and Affiliates Global.

I don't know what my job is.

I mean, I kind of know what I do day to day. Like what I'm supposed to be doing. But mostly I do nothing. Like maybe I do an hour's worth of actual work a day. I answer email. Fax signed forms and forms that need signing. Forward messages to my managers. Shit like that. And screening. All sorts of screening. I like screen calls and emails. Personal and business. I'm like a secretary, I guess. But most of the day I'm like on Assbook or downloading music or ordering shit online with the company account.

I got the job through a temp agency. I kind of like checked off all the boxes for work experience and training and shit so that I had a better chance of getting hired. And so far so good. After about a year I'm still working. Only problem is, I don't know what the hell we do. I guess maybe we're like some consultation company or whatever? Like maybe investments? I don't know. I don't really understand any of it.

Our website says shit like *we provide innovation... global clientele... competitive advantage... our winning circle... competitive vacuum... our industry leading services... beacon... murky waters... ability to shift in rapidly changing times...* I'm convinced we're good at what we do, only I don't know what that is. And I figure that after a year of working here, I'd sound like a fucking retard if I asked someone what it is we do at Petrus Cheong and Affiliates Global.

Anyway, the pay is pretty good and the work's easy. And everybody likes me.

But I mean, if I could like quit tomorrow, if I could do anything, my dream job would be like secretary at *Elle* or *Vogue* or *Cosmo*. And like maybe one day, I'd impress someone. Like one of the editors. I'd make a really smart comment or suggestion. Or have like a really cool idea. And my immediate bitch supervisor would like knock it down and make an ass out of me. Make me look like a real shit head. Because she hates me. And is like probably intimidated by me—because really she's insecure and stressed out and on pills. Like she's bipolar or some shit. Only the editor would find out about my idea and think it was brilliant. And then my cunt supervisor would like try to take credit for it. Go behind my back. Only the truth would come out eventually, and bitch gets fired, I get hired. And then they'd like give me a sex advice column, or maybe a relationship advice column or some shit.

But like I said, it's a dream job. They only hire skinny little bitches and the gays at those fucking rags anyways.

So I phoned work and told Brenda that I was puking all morning, which wasn't a lie, and she was all like, You get better, dear. You just rest and drink some ginger ale and get better. And I told Brenda that I would, and thanks, and that I'd see her tomorrow.

But still no call from Robert. He'd call, though. I was sure of it. It was only the morning—he was still sleeping. But honestly, I didn't really care. I just needed a shower. I just needed to wash all the puke out of my hair. And to brush my teeth. To brush the shit off my breath. Just too fucking gross.

And I really needed a coffee. A Venti. Two Ventis. And some ibuprofen. And to go back to sleep.


## Starbucks


I was shaking my head, I was so annoyed. Is this no fat whip? You're sure? *Three times.* I asked her like *three times* because I was watching her and I could *see her* grab the wrong whip. Ya ya, she says, it's the right one. And I'm like walking home across the visitor parking lot, drinking this shit, and I swear to god it's just regular fucking whip. And I can't deal with this and it's just too bright out, and I kind of pause and turn, like I'm confused, like I want to go back and throw it in her lying bitch face while it's still hot. Only I don't, I just turn to walk again and wish breast cancer on her. And that's when I see it, right in front of me. My Escalade.

It was parked crooked in one of the visitor spots. I felt like I'd just won the lottery. Honestly, the best feeling in the world is relief. It really is. Like scratching an itch, or taking that piss you were holding for an hour. Or having an orgasm. Like finally getting the results back and you're hep free. Or finding your Escalade after a bender. It's all like a release. Like relief. And nothing feels better.

But what the hell happened? I could barely remember the last couple of days. I remembered this morning. Waking up on the bathroom floor naked by the shitter. I remembered being up like half the night puking. And I don't know if maybe it was like a dream, but I think I remember looking in the bowl and seeing a finger before it got flushed.

And I know what started it all. It was this old lady at work. Like a retirement party. For Frona. She has an old fashioned voice and diabetes. Like she's going blind and shit. She's maybe forty-five, fifty. I hate her perfume. We took her out and got her drunk on her last day.

And I'd like to think that I had something to do with her chasing her dreams. Like I was a certified life coach. I convinced her that her time was too short to be wasted in a shit hole like Petrus Cheong and Affiliates Global. I asked her, Is that computer screen the last thing you want to see? The last thing you see before you go blind? I must have talked to her for an hour. Easy. I was all like, What about all those places you want to go to? The ones you're always talking about? All the things you want to experience? The cities and culture and natural wonder and all that shit? I didn't know what the hell I was talking about. I mean, I barely know her. But I couldn't stop.

So she was going to travel the world. Was off to Africa in a week to climb some mountain and go on a safari. Shoot some elephants or giraffes. I don't know. Maybe she was going to help build a bridge for some AIDS children. Whatever. All I knew was that I thought I'd parked my car and was going to catch a lift or a cab ride home. But I guess I drove. Oh well. No new dents. No animals or children sticking out of the grill. No worries. I didn't care what happened. I was just stoked that I found my car.

So I called 911. The dude asks me my name and my emergency, and I'm all like, No, there's no emergency, I'd just like to report my car unstolen. And I could just tell he was like annoyed, because he gives one of those loud frustrated exhales, like he was all rolling his eyes or shaking his head in disgust. And then he tells me to hang on—he's putting me on hold—he'll put me through to the police department.

I didn't even have to wait a minute, and someone answered. Maybe it was the same chick from yesterday. And I explain to her that I'd reported my car stolen last night. And could she please tell me how to like go about reporting it unstolen? So she starts laughing and asks me my name and all that shit and I answer her questions.

I make up lies about how my boyfriend borrowed it without my knowing. Like it was an emergency. He needed to drive a friend's sick dog to the vet. Like it got into some chocolate or antifreeze. And there was like dogshit, like diarrhea, all over the back seat. He tried to wash it out, but it still reeked—I was going to kill him. But the dog's ok, I tell her. And she just keeps laughing. Unstolen, she says. And I could just picture her shaking her head in like amusement or something on the other end. I liked this lady. And I knew that she liked me and wanted to help me. I make friends real easy.

So I get off the phone with my new friend, and see the message.

Boo
guess we need 2 talk. meet at our spot? 3 ok?

# Double Down

I got to KFC early. Robert is always late so I figured I'd see him in maybe a half hour. I wanted to make sure that I grabbed our booth. That everything would go right. Maybe this wasn't my last shot at saving our love, but I wasn't like taking any chances.

The idiot in front of me wasn't helping any. I hated him. There's always one. They're all the same. The retard who stands in line for like ten minutes and still doesn't know what he wants. Like he couldn't bother looking at the fucking menu while he was waiting. Like he's a machete-attacked-village African orphan or some shit and has never been to the KFC before. And you know that for sure he's going to ask absolute shithead questions. Like can he get bacon instead of lettuce on his Double Crunch Sandwich? Substitute chicken fries for regular fries? For the same price. What a douche. Like the world revolves around him. And he always whines that the fucking price has gone up since the last time he was there, like the teenager listening to his shit is Colonel Sanders.

I feel like sticking his face into the deep fryer. Or asking the tightwad if he wants a dollar. Like if it will shut him up and make him feel better. But I just can't be bothered. Maybe next time.

When it's finally my turn I order a six piece combo with slaw, fries, biscuit and Mountain Dew for Robert. His usual. And I order chicken strips, BBQ baked beans, crispy chicken Caesar salad, a Pepsi, and a Double Down with two sides of gravy for myself.

The Double Down is what the idiot in front of me should've been ordering. Every place has got one of them. It's an off menu item that's in the system. Only they don't display it on the menu because some people think it's disgusting. But I don't care I fucking love them. There's like a button for it on the till. It's like a secret code. They'll know what you're talking about. Except for like maybe the new or stupid cashiers.

The Double Down is two chicken fillets, bacon, and Monterey Jack slathered in the Colonel's sauce with no bun. Sort of like the Land, Sea and Air Burger at McDonald's—a McHamburger patty, Filet-O-Fish and McChicken patty with special sauce on a bun. Fucking gross. And embarrassing to order. Except for like maybe the most shameless of fat pigs. But I don't care, it's worth it. It's like our Secret. You just have to know how to ask for it. Sometimes you have to get out of your comfort zone, like go to extreme measures, to get what you want in life. To live full on.

And this was my cheat day. You've got to have your cheat days. Like reward yourself. I'm like Oprah's biggest fan. Ever. I love Oprah. I could go on and on about how much I love her. The billions of dollars she's made, her struggle with weight, the things she does for people, the list is too long. She should be president, or like a Pope or Dalai Lama or some shit. Seriously. She is like an amazing person. And Oprah knows what I'm talking about. Me and Oprah are into being conscious eaters.

What me and Oprah and Eckhart Tolle understand is that you have to bring a higher level of awareness to your eating. It's like, food is not there for you to stuff your face with any time that you're feeling crazy or depressed or emotional. You can't fill those kinds of holes with food. I have prescription medication to deal with my emotions. Food is like a decision. You should make healthy choices and know about the food you're going to eat. And you should enjoy your food, not just inhale it like some fucking fat kid left alone in a room with cake.

But a cheat day is very important. It's like a conscious decision. Like part of conscious eating. Where you say to yourself, You know what? You've been eating what you're supposed to be eating. Local, organic, fair trade, cruelty free. All that shit. And like helping fight corporations and politicians and globalization. Helping save the environment and the planet and shit. Doing everything you should be doing. So now you deserve a treat. A reward. Like you can spend a day eating as much of whatever the fuck you want. Just force-feed yourself. Binge. Because you and Oprah and Eckhart Tolle understand that sometimes, you deserve it.

I missed the last week's cheat day because of my cleanse. And I didn't really include the binge drinking as a cheat day because that's like a special occasion that I had no control over. And you can't just like say to people, No—I'm not going to your going away party because it's not my cheat day. That's like fucking ignorant. Like selfish. So I figured I was allowed a good cheat day. I mean, you have to live in the moment.

I found our table. Some ugly girl with freckles and braces was hovering around looking for a place to sit and I just gave her a nasty glare and sat down. This booth was special. It was our booth. Me and Boo always sat here. I gave him a handjob here, even.

So I just sat and ate and waited. I was kind of nervous. Excited.

I finished dipping the last of my Double Down into the gravy and threw the wrappers onto the floor under the table behind me. And there was Robert. He was about to go into the lineup. I smiled and waved for him to come over. He was wearing his white *Throwdown* shirt with all the sequined silver tribal designs and skulls on it. The one that said *Unbeaten. Unbowed.* And his baggy jeans. He only had the one pair but they were like perfectly stained and distressed. He had on his Docs. And his dark hair was like cut real short for the summer. He looked so hot.

Robert sat down and was all like, Hey, thanks for ordering for me. And he asks if I want some chicken because all I had left was a bit of salad, and I was all like, No, I'm not hungry. I'm good. I'm fine with salad, thanks.

And so he shoves some fries into his mouth and squirts ketchup onto his chicken and he's all like, Uhhh... so you're uh, so you're pregnant? You're like, uh, you're sure that you're pregnant? And I was all like Ya, I'm sure that I'm pregnant. And then he's like, But I uh, I thought you were on the pill?

And I can see where he's going with this, and it just annoys me, so I'm all like, Ya, I am on the pill, but I guess it didn't work, huh? So we're both sitting there all quiet and he keeps eating and then he goes, Well, uhhh... what do you want to do? Like, uh, what were you thinking... what are you planning on doing?

And I can totally tell that he wants me to abort. That he'd go out and steal the clothes hanger if he had to. Like if he had a car, he'd drive me to some Chinatown tattoo parlor restaurant where they performed abortion on the side. And then he asks if there's a morning after pill or something that I could take—have I thought of that? And if I'm sure that it's his.

And I just gasped. Like I was shocked. My mouth just dropped open like a retard's. I couldn't believe that he would even ask me something like that. For real? And I just started to tear up, I wasn't even faking. And my voice was all like quavery and loud and I was all like, What? Are you fucking serious? Really? Fine! If you don't want to take responsibility for this, then... then fine... You can just fuck off. Alright? Just fuck off. That's what you wanted anyways? Right? To fucking dump me? Well you know what? I don't even want your help with our baby. I'll fucking do it all by myself. I don't need your goddamn shitty help.

And then he finally stops staring at his fries for a second and looks at me. And he touches me, like just barely touches my fingers. And then he says sorry. So I keep crying and I lean into him, like we're hugging across the table. And I'm getting gravy and shit on my tits and I don't even care. He just keeps consoling me, like all gentle and quiet, like he's not even saying anything, just hugging. And it doesn't matter—he doesn't have to say a word. I know I've got him right where I want him.

# TP

I don't know if it was like the cleanse or whatever, but I totally had to take a shit. I insisted on giving Robert a lift to work, and he was already waiting in the SUV. Gary-Joe Noblett's foot was falling off or whatever, so Robert took his late shift for him. It was the least he could do, he said. Everybody liked Gary-Joe. His coworkers and the customers were like really pulling for him. They raised some money to help with medical bills. Like with change jars and bowling or some shit. Robert is always thinking about others that way. That's just the kind of guy he is. I'm like so glad that we're back together again.

Anyways, I fucking hate using public washrooms. They are absolutely disgusting. I get so grossed out when I think of like all the germs and shit and piss. And really, what kinds of people use these things? Just way too nasty. Just so fucking gross. But this was an emergency. So I like laid the toilet paper on the seat and sat down.

When I finished, I grabbed the roll of toilet paper and put it in my handbag, and I washed my hands. My hair and makeup looked fine, even after getting all teary. Then I took my log, which I had wrapped in the tissue, and dropped it in the sink. It landed perfect. Like the leaning Tower of Pisa.

I ran the dirty wad of TP under the tap, and threw it hard at the mirror. I washed my hands again and left quick before anybody else came in.

# Little Hussies

I'm not a religious person, But I am spiritual. It's like, I don't believe in anything, but I do believe there is something. I know a lot of people say that these days. Like it's popular. But I was like that way before they started saying it. Like before it became like all trendy.

I consult my cards and numbers online. I am a Nine, which makes me like a nurturing personality, which is so true. The most spiritual people—and usually the best people—are all Nines. We're like compassionate and idealistic. Like we care deeply for the world. You can probably guess famous Nines without even printing their names and doing the math.

I drew my cards. And I was like, for real? I can't believe how accurate these things are, it's scary. I drew The Wheel, The Queen of Cups, Three of Cups, The Empress, Ace of Wands, Star, and Nine of Pentacles. I might as well have started shopping for baby clothes.

And I almost did. I looked at pregnancy sites for hours, and I googled all sorts of pregnancy shit. What are the best foods to have smart babies? What are the best foods to have healthy babies? What are the best foods to have sexy babies? Can baby get my std? Most popular children clothing. Maddox baby clothes. Angelina baby clothes. Popular baby strollers. Popular cribs. Gwyneth baby care. Do babies have finger and toe nails when born? Baby yoga. Baby Pilates. Baby massage. Psychic connection to baby. Vegan baby food. Organic baby food. Toddler beauty pageants. Baby names. Best babies. Stop baby crying. Is it safe to give baby alcohol? Baby models. How do I get my baby into modeling? How do I get my baby into acting? Pill for hard odorless shit.

I can't believe how wrong I was. I've always hated children. Especially babies. Always crying. Always shitting. Draining your money. No more going out. No more time to yourself. Having the kid was like the end of your life.

I mean, that was all true, but having a kid—having a family—looked like a lot of fun. There were so many hot young couples out there with kids these days. It wasn't like you had to be a fat old housewife to have one anymore. And you know what? I wondered—why did I wait so long to have a baby? What was I so afraid of? I was pretty sure that this was what I always really wanted, without knowing it. This was going to be perfect.

The day just flew by and I was almost off work. I looked at some baby shit on YouTube. There was a couple of toddlers, like two or three years old, in their slutty ginch. Singing Fergie. Singing Lady Gaga. Katie Perry. I guess they weren't bad. But I thought to myself—my baby can do better. My baby can sing better than those little hussies.

Now I've just got to get pregnant.

# Muffintop

It's not as if I couldn't pull off pregnancy. I get pregnant real easy. I was even mistaken for being pregnant once.

I was like out drinking with some girlfriends at Globall one night. I wasn't seeing anyone at the time. And I'm like wearing this tiny half top and these supercute low riser jeans with no thong. I was looking hot. Like porn star hot. And I see this guy that I went to school with a couple years before. I start talking to him and I don't think he recognizes me. So I'm all like, Remember? I sat beside you in Remedial Math 11? I had Mr. Pappadopoulos fired for inappropriate touching? Dirty detention? Blindfold Fridays? The pylon? And it takes a few more details, but finally he's all like, Ohhhh, ok. I think I remember you now.

And so we start having like this really awesome conversation about shit we were doing after grad. And I kind of keep getting in closer because it's like loud, and we're talking loud, and I'm pulling the hair over my ear and leaning right into his face to hear him. And I'm moving my shoulders with the music, sucking on my straw, giving him the eyes. I start grinding him a little.

And things are like going so good, and then he says to me, How long before you have your baby?

And I'm all like, What? And I pull back. And retard leans in like he's going to ask again, and I cut him off, and I'm like, I *know* what you said! I was like stunned. And then I'm all like, Motherfucker!... Excuse me?... Are you fucking *joking*? Like seriously? Are you trying to be funny or something? And I'm like gaping and I feel like I'm going to cry, and then I'm all like, Fuck you! I'm not pregnant, dirtybitch... who the fuck do you think you are talking to people like that anyway?

And then I start going on about how I'm probably like bloated because I just ate at the Manna Garden, how it must have been all the carbs. And my period. How I was like retaining water because of my period. And that I'd been drinking a lot, like tons. And he just kind of shrugs, and shakes his head and is all like, Whatever, I said sorry.

But I keep going on about why I might look bloated, and he cuts me off and is like, Look... I just don't think it's appropriate for someone to be dressing that way and hanging out in bars when they're pregnant is all I'm saying...

And then some skank, his girlfriend, goes up to him and starts talking in his ear. I guess she's getting all jeal ous that her man's talking to some hottie at the bar. And I can sort of hear what she's saying a bit, like, Who is that? What does muffintop want? And then he's all like, I dunno, she's just some crazy pregnant chick who thinks we dated in high school.

And I really don't remember what happened next. My lawyer had it all thrown out of court anyways. Like they moved or didn't fill out some forms or shit. And I don't care what the witnesses said—I'm pretty sure that he shoved me first. But I guess that I like grabbed a pint glass and smashed it over the little whore's head. And she's all like screaming and her blonde hair's soaked with beer and turning red pretty fast and he's like trying to calm her down.

Then he turns to me and is all like shrieking, whining, Are you fucking crazy? What the fuck's the matter with you, you crazy bitch? And he turns back to her, like to calm her down, and he pulls off his shirt off and sticks it on her head. And she screeches more because I guess she's got glass stuck in her scalp. So he's ignoring me, and I grab a pool cue and crack it across his head real good. And by then the security's on me. She winds up with like twenty stitches, and he's got a concussion or a fractured skull or some shit and suddenly he's not talking so fast anymore.

And for like, I don't know, six weeks after that, I didn't eat. I puked yellow acid and bile and dry heaved. I ran up and down my stairs until my clothes didn't fit. Which kind of sucked because I had a lot of awesome clothes. But like a month later they all fit again, so whatever, it was all good.

## Prego

Heard you're prego. Thought you were looking a little bigger. Congratulations.

He didn't even look away from the tv for a second. He didn't even say hi. He just kept playing his retarded video game. Something where he was like running around and shooting and getting shot at. I wished the tv would really shoot him. Right in the balls. I can't fucking stand Dean Geoffrie Wheat.

So I was all like friendly, smiling, and I say to him—It's

true. Pretty exciting stuff. Guess you're gonna be Uncle Dean.

The thought made me sick. It made me sick to even talk to him. He was just sitting there like a slug on the couch. Like a sack of lazy pigshit. With his wifebeater and baggy jeans. His gold chains and rusty Caesar haircut. The 4:20 tattoo on his neck. So gross. Just so nasty.

Guess you gotta stop drinking so much, he says.

I didn't even bother responding—I would've smashed his stupid face in. So I was like, Hey Dean... is Robert around? And then he's like fucking ignoring me. And I'm about to ask him again and then he's all like, You flank the right. I'll take the rear... I'm good at taking the rear. And then I'm like confused. And he just starts laughing. His horrible weasel laugh. Hyuh hyuh hyuh. Showing his chipped teeth. Hyuh hyuh hyuh. I seriously wanted to puke. And then I like realize that he's talking to some other player on his headset, like I'm not even in the room.

And I'm like, Dean—I'm supposed to pick up Robert for work. Did he leave already? Did he just pop out? Is he coming back?

And I swear to god—I couldn't believe it. He takes his hand off his controller for a second and raises it to me. Like telling me to hold on. Like to wait. Like he's shushing me like I'm some fucking child. And he keeps talking some dumb video game bullshit to the nerd on the other end.

I don't even know why Robert lets him stay at his apartment. He's not even like his roommate. He just sleeps on the couch. He's supposed to pay Robert a couple hundred bucks a month. At least he told him he would. But he's like one of those assholes who always puts off paying his debts. Or he'll like bring up how he paid for a round, or a bag of weed, and somehow they're even. Just a total leech. Fucking gingerknob.

And he'll eat all of Robert's groceries. And never pay. He's not shy about using the last of something. He'll like literally squirt half a bottle of Quik into his glass of milk and leave nothing for Robert. The guy's a thoughtless douche. A total scumball. One time when I was going to the Circle K for smokes, he asked me to grab him a corn dog and a Polar Pop. Says he'd pay me later. So I grabbed that fucking corn dog for him. I grabbed it and dropped it on the ground. I dropped it in the ash bin. And I ran it under the rim of the toilet in the shitter. He said thanks when I got back. Asked if I wanted a bite. No... No I was good.

I guess Dean got shot. Like in his video game. He was all like, *No no no no no no no... aw fuck!—Fuck!—Jesus fuck Mary...* and then he finally answers me. Robert was late for work. He was supposed to be there a couple hours ago. He just ran out, just left. And I wondered why Robert wouldn't have called me? Like, hey—don't worry about the ride. And then I saw his cell on the kitchen counter. So I grabbed it and I started to leave. And I was all like, Alright, thanks Dean. I'll see you later... If you hear from Robert, tell him I'll still pick him up?... Alright?... Ok, see ya.

I hated to even say anything to that weasel. The greasy bastard. He was like just ignoring me. Can't even say bye. For real—he should be out on the street. He should be living in prison. Living with some big nigger horse cock up his ass. Rent free and hustling for cigarettes. I wished he'd die. Seriously, I just wished he'd choke on cock and die of AIDS, that fucking faggot.

And then I was leaving. I had the door open, and he goes, Oh hey, uh... got an extra cigarette? That fucking scammer probably has a full pack. He always does that. What a fucking bum. Fucking parasite. I bet he probably tries to convince Robert to sell our baby online, split the profits. He'd pimp his own sister and jerk off in the corner if he could. And I'm like, No, sorry Dean. Quitting. You know, baby and all.

And as I'm shutting the door, I'm not a hundred percent, but I swear I hear him go,

You got something on your pants. Looks like period.


## Juicy


Holy shit. My head was like spinning. He was right. Right below the Juicy on my white sweats. It wasn't there when I bought it. The red splotch. The red splotch that looked like I shit blood. My period.

I can't even describe the panic I felt. It was like the dream where you have the test you didn't study for. Or the one where you forget to wear clothes. It was like shitting your pants in public. Or getting caught by mom with a finger up the dog's asshole. I couldn't just swing the door open again and start babbling some lame excuses. It would be too obvious. He was going to tell Robert for sure, I knew it. Like it was some big joke.

When I was a little girl, I used to lie a lot. Like all the time. I'd lie about anything. I'd make up stories about friends I didn't have. If I broke the lamp it was never me. It was one of my friends. Anything and everything, I'd lie. I'd lie so much I believed my lies. At first my mom and my stepdad thought it was cute. But as I got older and lied to cover up for the bad things I did, like for my expensive mistakes, my illegal mistakes, my mom thought it was not cute. Like so not cute.

She had a saying. I don't know where it's from. Maybe the Bible? It was The wicked flees when no man pursueth. I didn't know what the hell it meant at the time, only that it meant mom was mad at me. And that I should probably start lying. Later I figured out that it meant like, the more you deny something before you even get blamed for it, the more likely you're lying. And more important—the more guilty you look. So I learned to lie only when I got blamed, and not before. And to lie right the first time. Lie once and lie right.

So I like calmed down. The wicked flees when no man pursueth. I wasn't going to say another word to Dean. The lady doth protest too much. That was the other one. My mom read a lot of the Bible or some shit. I'd just let it slide. Like nothing happened. Dean's a fucking retard anyways. He's sneaky. He's like street smart. I'll admit that maybe he's even cunning. But he's a shithead. Fucking stupid. Stupid and ugly. I don't even think he like knows what period is, except that he finds it funny. I just hoped he wouldn't mention it to Robert.

It didn't matter anyways. Within a couple of weeks I'd be knocked up. That was for sure. Then it wouldn't matter what the fuck that retard said. I would just say that it was lies. Lies straight from hell. Give him a ride to Crazytown—he's fucking nuts. Or maybe I'd just mention something to Robert in passing. Like you wouldn't believe what I sat on. I'd think of something, I always do. It would be fine. I had all day to think of shit.

I threw an empty BK bag and napkins on my car seat before I sat down. Now I was just annoyed. This was the last time I used these expensive bullshit hemp tampons. *Fatties—The Green Tampon*. Organic even. Whatever. I looked at Robert's phone, at the wallpaper of fifty dollar bills fanned out across a fake set of tits. I was going to visit him at work, drop off his cell, see if he needed a lift home later. Right after I popped in a new plug and changed my pants. Right after I checked every number on that phone. Checked every number and every goddamn message.


## Cousin Terry


I couldn't believe it. Like was he for real? Seriously? There was no fucking way. So I was all like are you kidding me? Is this some kind of sick joke? Seriously—I thought he was fucking joking. For like an hour, I thought he was messing with me. I nearly raped him a half dozen times before I finally realized he wasn't shitting me. It was insane. Robert would not have sex with me. Not while I was pregnant, he said.

Why? Why the fuck wouldn't he have sex with me? It wasn't like I was any bigger. It's not like he could poke the baby in the eye. It was like maybe a month old—or at least he thought so. What the hell was his problem? So I told him this was his last chance. That I wouldn't put out for another week if he kept trying to be funny. But he was firm. He wouldn't do it.

He wasn't trying to be an asshole, and he really didn't want to talk about it, he said. But I was furious. Except I was faking like I was all sad—like I was upset that he wasn't attracted to me anymore. Only really I wanted to punch him in the face, to bust his fucking nose, and ask him, ask him while he bled, Why? Why not? Is it that... that little bitch? You'll fuck around with some other cunt behind my back and now I'm not good enough?

I wanted him to know that I knew. That maybe you shouldn't leave messages from other bitches on your cell. That maybe you shouldn't leave your cell lying around where I could find it—where I could find it and listen to those messages and read every shitty text. But whatever—that could wait. I wasn't about to let that little whore get between me and my man. I wasn't going to let her fuck this up.

So he apologizes again and says it's not me, it's not what I'm thinking. So I kind of cheer up and I'm all like, Come on, you're being an idiot. This is just retarded. You're being a fucking retard. And then he looks at me all serious and says, That's it. That's why. He says that he's sorry, but he doesn't want a retarded baby.

And I start laughing. Like I couldn't believe it. I never knew he was so funny. I couldn't stop. And he just shakes his head and rolls his eyes and turns over, like he knew that's how I'd react. So I was still laughing and I was all like, What? Come on, don't be that way—you were joking, right?

And he just ignores me and reaches to the nightstand for a cigarette. And finally I calm down enough to tell him that he's wrong. That he's being crazy. That a baby can't turn retarded that way. Only now I'm not so sure, and a little worried that he's right—and absolutely horrified that I could have a retarded baby.

And he says that it's true, that he didn't want to add more sperm. Like add more chromosomes or DNA or extra baby or whatever. He says that it's happened before. That it was a medical fact. That it happened to his cousins. His mother and Auntie Pattie told him so. Their sister Donna had retarded babies.

Cousin Terry was bowlegged and cross-eyed because Uncle Russ kept fucking Auntie Donna right up until he accidentally induced birth. And the same thing happened to Cousins Leo and Cliff. It was in the papers, like on the news. They were like conjoined at birth, and had to be separated from the hip and part of their sides. Like they shared a spleen or some shit. And now they're all like crooked and short and walk weird. Like they limp and shake a leg a couple times with every step. All lopsided and gross. It looks really weird, and they look really weird. Like little kids stare at them.

And it's not like they can get work, because they're all crooked and gimpy, or bowlegged and cross-eyed. And Robert says the twins are drunks and addicts and spend whatever's left of their welfare and government disability checks on prostitutes. And if they need more drug money they'll like sing in their froggy voices and dance on street corners. He thinks Cousin Leo plays tambourine. And Cousin Terry huffs paint fumes behind a Taco Bell dumpster most days so that he can see straight. All because Uncle Russ and Auntie Donna couldn't control their horniness during pregnancy.

And then he tells me about like a second cousin of his or something. Lorne. He's like one of those smart retards who can like remember the phone book or some shit. Wears glasses even. He's not sure if Lorne's parents kept fucking while they were pregnant with him. But Robert says he strongly suspects that they did.

And it's like, now I'm not so sure about having kids with Boo anymore.


## Downward dog


I started sucking cock when I was ten. Maybe eleven. So I'm pretty good at it. I ran with some pretty hot bitches back in Junior High and High School. It was a lot of competition. *A lot* of competition. So I had to work a little harder to stand out. I had this trick where I would like take a banana and shove it all the way down my throat, then pull it back out. It was like an advertisement. Like it said, This girl is really good at gobbling knob, and will probably put out. Which was like true. And it worked.

Robert wouldn't fuck me, but he'd still let me blow him. And if he wasn't going to give me what I needed to have his baby, I was going to take it.

I got the idea from tv. I was like flipping around, and there was one of those nature shows on. Like this one about birds. Crows. And they showed like all these clips, and these nerds were all like going on about how smart the birds were and how they lived. And they were like filming this one bird. A mother. And they showed the mother bird feeding her baby birds. Like all chewed up worms or some shit. It was fucking gross. And I guess they were like watching the bird too much. And she like took off. Or was like eaten by a cat or whatever. So these scientists sort of adopted these baby birds, and fed them like blender worms with some sort of puppet bird and an eye dropper.

And I'm like watching this, and then I knew. I knew what I had to do. And it's like, I'm not religious, but I am very spiritual. And I felt this deep like, connection, I guess. To the world. I've read and listened to a lot of books. Books like *The Secret*. Seriously—I am a Secreteer. For real. So it's like, I know how to get what we want. I know all about manifesting what we desire into our lives. And I wanted Robert. And to keep Robert, I wanted and needed a baby. The universe is huge. You just ask it for something and it'll like give it to you. And so this was like the universe giving me a hint. Pointing me to my baby. You just have to be like open to the signals. You have to accept the gifts when they're given.

So I was at Robert's, and I'd just finished him off. And I went to him something like, Aw gawdoo go... awl be rawd bawk... and I went to the shitter. And it was exciting, like I was a chemist. Like some kind of biologist. Like a famous dog breeder. Maybe even like one of those chipmunks or squirrels or some shit.

I took the soap dish and spat Robert's load into it. It was a fair bit. Half our baby. I grabbed my hidden turkey baster from behind the toilet. Like one of those smaller ones. Then I tried sucking Boo's goo into it, but the baster was still too big, like there was too much air in it. So I ran a bit of water until it was like room temperature, and splashed a bit into the dish. It worked.

I didn't even notice until after I'd done it. And I'd like to think that what happened next was like maybe out of my Sense of Sacred, but I don't know. Without thinking about it, I rolled into a shoulder stand lotus pose. Queen of Asanas, or like one of the queens. As my yoga instructors Siobhan and Eiohan would say, it promotes proper thyroid function, strengthens the core—especially the abs and lower back—elongates the spine, improves circulation, and helps relaxation. And I honestly don't know what the thyroid is or does, except that if it doesn't work your eyes get all buggy, but Siobhan and Eiohan could add self-insemination in a tight spot to that list. Like four-hundred square-foot filthy bachelor pad shitter tight.

I inserted the turkey baster into my cunt, and squeezed the life into my womb. Boo's spew. Half our baby. And it's like I felt electricity. Like a jolt. It was like that picture in that church of god and a man touching fingers. Like I was transformed into some kind of Madonna or some shit. Like immaculate conception. Like when the aliens abduct and knock up depressed lonely women who lie for attention. It was the most alive and the most calm or serene that I can ever remember being. Maybe it was all the blood rushing to my head, maybe it was the baster in my vagina, but it was like bliss.

And then I hear Dean rolling into the apartment. Probably back from the Wal-Mart. Done rubbing his crotch against women for the day. For real, he was like a suspect—like he was investigated for that. A truck was stolen and left in a Wal-Mart parking lot. The security cameras picked up a man who exited the truck, entered the store, and repeatedly rubbed his crotch against female shoppers and a couple of employees. There was like maybe eight all together. The man got away. And then it happened again a few weeks later, at a different Wal-Mart. Security caught him that time, but he swore up and down it wasn't him. They couldn't do anything about it. Too many guys in hoodies, and the video was too grainy and shitty. I mean, seriously, why do these places even have cameras? But I swear to god he did it. He's still not allowed in Wal-Mart, the fucking pervert.

Anyways, he starts shaking the knob, and I'm all like Shit, Dean... Just a second. And he's like, Hey, you gonna be long? I really gotta piss.

So I'm scrambling. I turn on the tap. Pull the baster out. Stash it behind the toilet again. Tidy shit up. And then he's knocking like a rude asshole.

What? Are you having the kid in there? Another period? Come on, man. Hurry the fuck up.

I wanted smash the toilet tank lid over his Caesar cut. Crack his fucking head open. Curb stomp his ugly chipped teeth onto the rim. But I was like, Just give me a second, Dean. And then I opened the door. He was standing in the entrance and stank like beer and weed. I just smiled and walked right by him to Robert's room and listened to him piss for like three minutes.

The moment was over. Dean had made sure of that. But I didn't care, I was done for the day.

I did the same thing five more times that week, just to be sure. It was like a ritual. Like a religious rite. With special attention to detail. The soap dish. The spitting. The baptism. The asana. The insertion. Conception.

I did try it once with the downward facing dog posture, but it just didn't feel right.

# Text Message to Gingerbox

roses r red
violets r blue
ur fucking dead bitch


# Lavafair

I guess word spread pretty quick about the slut in the Indian headdress. I wore a tiara and boa the first day, but half the little bitches in the Lavafair were wearing tiaras. I needed to stand out.

I wasn't going to like just trust my pregnancy to science. If Robert was going to be such a freak about it, I'd have to guarantee I got knocked up somewhere else. About twenty-five miles outside of town.

And I might have felt bad about it if Robert hadn't cheated on me. Hadn't dumped me. This was karma as far as I was concerned. I mean, I'm huge into Buddhism. Huge. I love the Dalai Lama and shit. I love him almost as much as I love Oprah. A friend of mine gave me his audio book *How To Deal With Anger* a few years ago, which I've listened to a hundred times. I've also read *The Art of Happiness*, and *How To See Yourself As You Really Are*. For real, I could be a Buddhist if I wanted to.

Anyways, it's been a few years since my clubbing days, my rave days. It's all a bit of a blur, really. I mean, specific things—weird details, ODs and whatever—pop out here and there, like shitty half-developed Polaroids. But really, it was all like a dream. Like me and a bunch of nameless, slutty ghosts drifted into these warehouses and clubs for the night, and then faded back into the city and our regular lives in the morning.

It didn't seem like much had changed, but I don't know, I couldn't fucking remember.

There was the darkness, the pulsing lights. Everyone was young and beautiful. At least with the foxy moxie and vodka they were. Chrome and glass and angles everywhere. The perfume and cologne. The waves of rising and falling beats. I was dancing, grinding like a ditch pig. Kissing guys, kissing girls—I'm a good kisser. I have a pierced tongue and full lips that I maintain with injections every six months. I was shameless, confident. Like a small town whore.

And the things you notice on your knees in the men's shitter. I remember *irish have stinky pussy* scratched into the stall more than I remember the guy I was blowing. And never mind stinky pussy, I remembered his smelly balls. At first I thought it might be the smell in the shitter, but I'm sure it was his balls. Maybe it was poor personal hygiene, or maybe it was because he was like dancing all night, but they stank real bad. It was fucking gross. I mean, I wasn't even going to blow him at first, but I was already down there, so whatever.

But I couldn't even finish, it stank so bad. So I just sort of got up and ran away. It wasn't like I was going to get knocked up by blowing guys anyways. I left to find some other dudes. It wasn't that hard. And before I knew it, my dirty weekend was just another blur.

I don't know—maybe it was just the drugs, but it felt like I'd done something spiritual. Like I'd taken part in something magical. Cycle of life or some shit. It's like so many animals, like in nature, have these narrow opportunities to mate. These tiny windows of real specific conditions. Spawning season, mating season. Those little fish that mate under the full moon at Orbit Beach every year, like clockwork. All those other animals on my nature dvds. Shit like that. And it was like—*I* was one of those animals now, like David Attenborough should have been narrating my weekend. I mean, I did all that I could, and now it was over. I was out of time.

But between my dates with the turkey baster and all the pervs at Lavafair, I was pretty sure that I was pregnant. For real—I was like the goddamn sperm bank for a week. Whether it was Boo, the short bald troll with the white glasses and Kangol cap, Paco Rabanne One Million in the silver shirt, the hairy eager guy with a small dick who made gross noises like a kitten, or Smelly Blowjob, one of them was going to be a father.

Well, except for Smelly Blowjob. But that was for the best, really. He was like mulatto or some shit anyways and I'd have a hell of a time explaining a brown baby.


## Red Bull


I woke up after six o'clock and I was like totally disorientated. I felt a jolt of panic, like I'd slept through my alarm and was going to be late for work. Only it was after work, and I was sleeping at work. Maybe I should have called in sick this morning.

I used up all my sick days though, so I really didn't want to call in and push my luck. Besides, my head wasn't throbbing and I wasn't like violently ill or whatever. It was one of those nice two-for-one hangovers where you feel high or stoned the next day. Those are awesome on a day off, but it sucks when you have to work. There was no way I could function.

But I did make it into the office. I was like sitting at my desk in my glitter and heavy makeup and drinking coffee and Red Bull and trying not to fall asleep. I had like six Red Bull and had to stop. If you have like eight Red Bull, your heart will explode. It's true. It happened to this one kid in like Germany or France or some shit. Maybe Sweden. He drank like eight Red Bull and had a jammer and died.

Anyways, I was struggling. I was a bit of a disaster. I got a call asking if Dave had gone for lunch yesterday. Who the hell was this? I didn't recognize the voice because it sounded like it was on speaker phone or some shit, and the phone was like showing Line 101 and not some extension. So I was like, Pardon me? And she asks me again if Dave had a lunch yesterday. I was like confused and tired and I wanted to cry. It's like, was this LaKeefa in payroll, was it Dave's wife, or someone else? I mean, it *sounded* like LaKeefa in payroll, only I couldn't tell for sure because it was on speakerphone and I didn't want to sound like a retard and ask who the hell is this? Then she asks if Dave is still in his meeting—and he was. Relief. This was my out. So I was like, Yes he is—do want me to leave a message? And she was like, No, could you just find out for me and call me back? Thanks, bye.

I felt like I'd never been more confused in my life. I just put my head down into my arms and cried and passed out. I was like dreaming of space, of Pegasus-sunsets on glass high-rises, and of some city that was like this one but was really like no city I'd ever been to before. I was hanging out with people that I really liked and they were doing important things. It was like reality had shifted on me, and maybe I was in a better world, where I had better friends and a better job and more money.

I snapped out of it. The phone was ringing, but I missed the call. Maybe it was LaKeefa again? I didn't care. I needed more coffee. Only when I got to the coffee machine, all the paper cups were gone. There were like a couple in the cupboard, but they looked like they were covered in pencil shavings, or like someone had farmed or planted shit in them. So I went to the supplies room. I think I needed more staples or post-it notes anyways.

I got there and it was like my head was floating, like an air retard or some shit. And I thought to myself maybe I needed vitamins, to eat some fucking fruit. I stood in the doorway, stunned for about a minute, trying to figure out what the hell I was doing.

Right. Paper cups. So I went to the far left corner where the cups were supposed to be. Nope. Not there. These idiots just throw shit wherever. I work with a bunch of animals. And maybe I took it too personally, but I hated them with a passion—I really had to find a cup. I looked across at the bottom right corner and thought I saw them tucked way back in the shelf, only I couldn't tell for sure, it was pretty dark.

And then it was like I was still in my dream. It was like

magic. Like the universe really did shift. Like it finally came around for me. *I* was the girl in the urban fantasy novel. I mean, for real—I'd been in there a hundred times before and had never noticed it—there was an opening behind the shelf.

It was like that story where those children open the wardrobe and go on adventures with the talking lion and the green elves and shit. Or that one with David Bowie and his tight pants and the crotch bulge and he steals the baby. Or like that movie where John Cusack crawls into the weird guy's head and has an amazing adventure. It was like a modern faery tale. Like Oz, like Og. A Kabbalah secret. Like something lost from childhood found. It was a dream where you win the lottery, but only it's for real.

Anyways, I was pretty excited. I felt like this deep connection to my childhood. I crawled under the shelf, like into some closet, maybe six feet by six? I don't know, I'm not fucking Jesus. But it was big enough to lie down in. And it was dark and warm. It was perfect. And somebody else knew this too because there was an air mattress and blanket.

I set the alarm on my phone for fifteen minutes and slept. I did this four times in the morning, and for an hour on my lunch. My desk was filled with rubber bands and paper clips by noon. This was turning out to be the best day at work.

Only I guess I fucked up the alarm on my last nap. Everybody was gone when I crawled out of my hole, except for some old Mexican lady and her husband who were like vacuuming. They ignored me when I went to my desk and signed out of work on the phone.

I smiled and waved at Guadalupe. I don't know her name. She turned off her vacuum, and I asked her if she'd let me out, all loud and slow so she'd understand. I explained to her that I had a lot of work to catch up on, that I guess I'd lost track of time. And I tell her that it's rough being the CEO of a company—that there's just not enough hours in the day. How I needed to get home to feed my daughter, and somehow find the time to get ready for a charity dinner that I'd organized. All after a fifteen hour work day. And I laughed and shook my head at her like I was crazy. She didn't say anything. It was pretty clear we had nothing in common, but whatever. I followed her to the door and she locked it after me on my way out.

## Retail boxes duking it out

I friended her on Assbook. I found out all about her. Looked at all her stupid photos. Read her wall. She thinks she's *In a Relationship*. I was going to teach that little cunt a lesson. Teach her what happens when she messes with another woman's man.

She was on Robert's ball team. His pub sponsored team. Like the one he and his work buddies play on. The one that he didn't want me playing on. Said he wanted some time for himself. Time with the guys. Time with the ball team sluts.

I couldn't believe I didn't see this. I trusted him too much. I felt like an idiot. Like a total shithead. I was convinced that all his friends knew. And all of his coworkers and their friends too. Talking about me behind my back. Laughing about me like I was a fucking joke. Or maybe feeling sorry for me. I don't know. Whatever, I didn't care. I hated them all. And I knew for a fact that Dean knew—and I hated him the most. He was one of her buddies on Assbook. I was in shock that he didn't tell me. I mean, it hurt, it really hurt—I was his friend too. Or at least he thought I was his friend. I felt so betrayed by Dean, and I hated him more than ever. I hoped to god he'd get hep. Get hep ABC and hit by a bus and die. I wouldn't forget this.

She saw me in the mirror, looking at her while she did her eyeliner.

She works at the bar. Robert's ball team sponsor. Day shift. I had a couple drinks and followed her into the shitter. She was like doing her makeup. I was behind her, just staring at her, like one of those staring drooling retards. God, I felt like puking. I was sick. This is what he's attracted to? He cheats on me with this? This is what he couldn't control himself over? This frecklepuss? This skanky gingerbox? Just so gross. Just too fucking nasty. I mean, she wasn't a full on ginger, with like the dirty orange dishwater Brillo pad hair. And she was sort of pretty I guess. She was skinny. But I was prettier for sure.

So she sees me and makes eye contact and is all like, Do you need to use the mirror?

There's all sorts of mirror—she's just being polite. I don't say anything at first, I just keep giving her a nasty look, and then I'm all like, Stay away from my man. And then she's like, What? You gotta speak up Sweetie, I can't hear you. So she turns around and is facing me. She's young, like early twenties. I hate that she calls me Sweetie. I don't like it at all. And I look her straight in the eye, and I'm like, Stay away from my man. Stay away from my man, you fucking cunt.

And she kind of laughs and shakes her head and looks like at me like I'm crazy, like she doesn't know what the hell I'm talking about. And then she's like, Um, I think you're confusing me with someone else. I have a boy-friend.

And then I get right up in her face. Real close. So close that I can smell her gum and notice that she doesn't have any freckles. That the bitch has flawless white skin that should like be on a soap commercial. And I get even more jealous and the hate is burning me and choking me and making me dizzy. And then I'm all like, I said stay away... Stay away from my man, you... you fucking cunt. Stay away or I'll... I will grab you by the back of your head and shit in your face. Do you fucking understand?

So she steps back and is all like, Jesus, calm down... quit screaming... I really think you've got me confused with someone else... I honestly don't know what you're talking about.

And I mean, what a joke. For real? Seriously? If she thought I was screaming, bitch is fucking crazy—I was so not screaming.

And then I laugh, and I think I'm like starting to cry. And I really can't hear what she's saying because all the blood is like rushing to my head and my ears are ringing. She's like pointing at my crotch and I'm not so sure, but I think she says something like, your camel toe's leaking. And it was true—I like peed my pants. And I wanted to say *Keep your skinny cunt away from my boyfriend*, or at least I tried to say it, but it was like one of those dreams where you try to scream and you can't make a noise. I'm pretty sure I was like hyperventilating.

So I just went at her. I kicked her in the box and grabbed her ginger hair with both hands and pulled her head down like to the side. And she's all like shrieking, Stop it! What are you doing? Fuck off! Leave me alone! Fuck off! And then she's like reaching with her claws and trying to grab my hair. But I'm like bigger and taller than she is and have reach. So I kind of pull her head into my side and struggle and get her into a headlock.

She's trying to push her head out but I've got her good and tight. And she's like desperate, with these pathetic little kicks, and I can feel her jaw moving at my side, like she's trying to bite my tit. And then she's pinching my arm, which actually kind of hurt. So I give her a couple shots to the face, and then kind of like use our momentum and crash her head into the stall. And then I get obsessed with the idea of pushing her face into the toilet.

But then bitch starts struggling more, and manages to like pull her head out. And she's bent over and kind of whipping her head back and forth like a dog with a chew toy or some shit. But I still got her hair, and I'm like pulling her blouse up over her head.

And then I stop.

Or really, it was more like time stopped. Like it stood still. For real, it was like Keanu Reeves. It was like I was the Matrix. Like I could see everything. And there it was. Right between her dimples. Right over her crack. Right over her perfect ass that stung me and made me hate her even more. My tattoo. My tramp stamp. I swear to god it was exactly the same. There was like kanji for *Magnificent* over top of *Love*, surrounded by a tribal design. And

for a second, it was like, this cunt that I was beating up—
it was like I was beating up me.

So I let go of her. I mean, I don't know why. I guess I
was just stunned. Like it was too weird. Like I saw myself.
What were the odds? The exact same tattoo? Like I was
fighting the sister I didn't have or some shit. My twin.
My bitch twin.

And then she like backs up and is all tangled in her
blouse. And then I see it. Her dangly bellybutton ring.
And I grab that fucking thing and pull. At first I just miss
it, like I couldn't get a grip. And she backs up all quick
into the sink, sort of bent over, still struggling with her
blouse. Finally she just pushes it off so she's just in her
bra. But it's too late. I get a good grip on the dangly and
yank. She screams and sort of falls to the floor. And I got
her dangly and I shove it into my mouth and swallow it.
Then I'm like standing over her, trying to catch my
breath. And I point at her and I'm all like, Keep your
skinny cunt away from Robert... or I'll... I'll cut you up... I
swear to god I'll cut your face you fucking bitch... You
tell him about this... I come back here and cut your tits
off... got that?

I owned her. Like I was a dangerous prison dyke, like
she was my bitch. And if she wasn't careful I'd rape her
with the dirty prison mop handle after I'd finished beating her with it.

And then I like hear the music get louder and some
laughing and the door swings open. A couple of chicks
walk in and they just stop. We're a mess. We must look
like a couple retail boxes duking it out in the shitter, like
some YouTube clip. And one of the girls must have
thought so too, because she puts up her phone like she's

going to film us.

So I pull the bear spray out of my jacket and spray them. They're like screeching. And I then I bear spray Gingerbox, and I rip the used tampon thing off the wall and throw it at her too. She's like all pathetic and crying on the floor. I really don't know what else to do and my eyes are like starting to sting, so I pick up the garbage bin and throw it at her. And I spit on her. And then I just run. I shove those shrieking bitches out of my way and I run like Flo-Jo.

I run for maybe like the first time since high school. And I bear spray the idiot bartender who always says Cheers after he serves you. And I bear spray Mike and Chloe, the cool young Aussie couple at the pool table who I shot a round with earlier. I bear spray the red faced old man with the gross pitted Karl Malden nose who's buying pull tabs and reeks like booze and pipe smoke. I bear spray the security camera at the exit. And then I run to the Escalade and drive the fuck away from that shit hole.

# TWO

# Risk

I handed Robert an orange from my handbag because I was getting sick watching those two eat. Like for real. Nachos with chili and cheese sauce, bean and cheese burritos, hot pockets stuffed with donkey dink, all sorts of chocolate bars, like twenty bags of candy. It's sick. And I can't help it. I tell them about the sugar, the gluten, the sodium, the chemicals. How all the shit they're eating is garbage. It's disgusting.

And I tell them about the diet I'm on, like for me and the baby. How I've got these supplements. Like açaí berry and organic greens, how I lose weight and the baby lives off my fat. And this sterilized dirt and civet manure slurry from the jungles of Sumatra that I was going to get. Loaded with colloidal minerals from the volcanic earth. Microbiotically balanced and shit. You eat a teaspoon a day and it helps with nutrient absorption—which is so important for a growing baby. And Dean's all like, Ya. That'll work.

Dean does not get it. He just does not get it. You know? He just doesn't understand. I can't believe the guy. I've dieted my whole life. I know a little bit about what I'm talking about. I'm trying to help him and he says shit like that. And Robert just laughs and peels the orange so that the rind looked like a dick.

Most of my armies were holed up in Kamchatka, so I could like escape into Europe or Alaska if I had to. I've been on the move, on the attack too much. I wasn't going to last much longer. We were playing Risk. I suck at games, but Robert and Dean wanted to play. I was pretty sure Dean was winning. He was hiding out in Australia, building up his armies.

The late news was on tv, and there was all sorts of miserable garbage. There was some shit about global warming, like they're interviewing idiots in the street. Some crazy bitch was going on about how it gets hotter every time they send shit into space. The other crybabies were boring, and they were whining about the same old bullshit. And then they tied that into the next story. Some Chinese shit hole or whatever just got hit by another typhoon. There was like footage of cars and houses and people being washed away. A million people were missing or dead or some shit. And I nearly cried I was so happy—they showed a dog and an ox that were rescued off a roof.

And Dean was all like, They're getting hit pretty hard out East. Earthquakes. A hurricane. Flooding... God must hate them... He's punishing them. Punishing those sodomizers... Fucking queers. Then he goes on about how he saw a couple dudes walking down the street holding hands on his way to the horse track. How he would have beat the shit out of them if he wasn't in such a hurry.

And then I go to him, So what? Who cares if they were holding hands? Big deal. So they like each other and want to hold hands. And I just shake my head in disgust and I'm all like, You're such a fucking racist sometimes.

And he was all like, Whoa. Didn't know your girlfriend was such a dyke, Robbie. And then he tells us that he's done his turn, and he moves all his armies from Indonesia into Southeast Asia, like he's positioning himself to move into China and Mongolia and Kamchatka to take me out. Destroy me. Knock me out of the game next turn. I would have cheated, but the cards and armies were across the table. And I don't think Robert's heard a word, and he was all like, Man... this is the sweetest orange I've ever eaten.

There was another story on the news, about some man who was like crippled and blind. It looks like his face was ripped off by a bear or was caught in a burning escalator or some shit. He drools and wheezes when he tries to talk about his stolen scooter. He's had a rough go, and the scooter and his guide dog have really made things less miserable for him. You can like barely hear or understand him he's wheezing and gargling so much. It sounds like his voice box has AIDS. There's like captions under him. Everyone agrees it's like a real tragedy. Whoever did it was a real piece of work, a real scumball. A stupid senseless crime, committed by cowards, the officer says. And anyone with information can call this number on the news, or the police department. Everything's anonymous. Gargler doesn't care about the stolen pension check, but he'd really like to get the scooter back.

Robert turned the channel. He was gagging. He says seriously—he can't eat with that shit on the tv, that it shouldn't be on there when people are trying to eat. And I guess he couldn't get it out of his head because he got up all quick to go puke. So Dean turned the news back on. It was pretty much finished. There was like some human interest story about some kid in a puddle, some bum in a junkyard, or some guy balancing on a fence or doing some stupid shit in the park. Maybe it was an old couple bragging about how they met, I can't remember.

So Robert got back and it was his turn. He attacked Dean. And he kept attacking but he kept rolling ones. Ones and twos. And it was like he wasn't even swearing—he wasn't saying anything he was so mad. He just kept shaking his head, like he was so disgusted, like the world was against him. And I swear—he rolled ones and twos like twenty times in a row. Maybe the world was against him.

But I mean, it shouldn't have been a big deal. He should have expected it. Dean always wins games, but that's because the guy's a cheating weasel. It's like his life depends on it. Like his life is a waking struggle where he needs to cheat and lie, to shuck and jive, or he'd get like beaten and killed and die in the ditch.

So me and Dean were like waiting for Robert's next move. And he was just looking at the board like he was in deep thought, like he was thinking. Like he's holed up in the Alamo, or Waterloo, or Hitler's bunker. And then he just swings his arm across the table and throws the board and the dice and all the little pieces across the room, and he was all like, Fuck this, I'm leaving. It was pretty sudden.

So Dean tells him to calm down, relax, it's only a game. Here, let's go on the deck and spark one up, he says. So they went onto the balcony and smoked a joint and I poured myself some vodka while they were out. When they got back in, we watched *Baraka* on dvd and everybody mellowed out. Me and Robert were on our couch, and Dean sank into his couch like some filthy animal. Like some filthy animal that would do three circles and scratch the dirt before it laid down in its own shit.

After *Baraka*, Robert was tired and wanted to go to sleep, which was fine by me, because I had to work in the morning and was sick of these guys anyways. And Dean said he had to get up early too—he had some appointment with his ambulance chaser.

Dean was like beaten pretty bad a few months back at some apartment complex. He was dealing and they stole his money and weed. At least that's the story he tells us. The police report says he was beaten and robbed by some young black men. A random mugging. But for real, I think he owed someone and he was overdue and they collected. But I don't know, whatever. I don't give a shit.

Anyways, because he can't get any money from the dudes who beat the shit out of him, he sues the owners of the apartment complex. For like having no security systems in place. Poor lighting. That kind of shit. He says that he tried to pull the fire alarm when he stumbled down the hall, but it didn't work. So his sleazy lawyer— who I think tested the alarms himself and told him to say that—figures he's got a pretty good case.

I was leaving and I looked at Dean. He was crashed out on the couch. Snoring. Even when he slept he still looked like a dude who would do anything to get by. Like he'd suck some old perv's cock for twenty bucks and then stab him with his rusty screwdriver. I fucking hated him, just lying there. All useless. His chipped snaggleteeth. His open eyes. And I wished he'd get raped. Raped by some mental hospital nigger who'd crawl through the window while he slept. I wished he'd get raped and dry fisted by that animal maniac and catch Hep A and die.

Or I could kill him. While he snored and drooled, I could kill him. Except for I'm not crazy.

But I'd be lying if I said that I didn't think of murdering him. Of smothering him. Of sitting on his ugly face and grinding him to death. He'd struggle and he'd scream into my fat ass. But it would be no use, because no one would hear him. No one but me.

And then I had this idea. I've got this crystal that I keep in my handbag. It's like attached to a string. And you hold it between your bird and your thumb and it'll like swing back and forth or in circles. You can ask it questions if you want. Or use it to find ley lines and faery circles if you're into that shit. But I like to use it to read people. Like their energy, their aura. We are all covered in chakras, which are like full of energy, and different energy affects the crystal in different ways.

So I held my crystal over Dean, and I swear to god, it like swung out and pointed right at him, like on a forty-five degree angle. I'm not even joking. Like he was a crystal magnet. And it started to swirl around real fast. Like a fan, clockwise. And when I pulled it away, it swirled in a tighter circle, even faster.

I don't think the crystal is supposed to act that way. I don't think it is like even scientifically possible. I've never seen that before. It was intense. And I don't really know what it means, but I think he like sucks energy from everywhere. Like the crystal was being sucked into his energy drain. His black hole. I believe Dean has no aura because it's like sucked into his asshole, what we yogas call the Kundalini.

This really explained everything. He was like a bad influence, like bad energy, always dragging Robert into his shit. He just wasn't the kind of guy you wanted to be around. I mean, he was the kind of guy who said tekillya instead of tequila. Every time. Like he was always saying it for the first time, like it always got funnier.

I knew I had to cut Dean out of our lives. It was like a priority. But I mean really, it was only a matter of time now anyways. With Boo and I starting a family, we'd have to move in together. Like, we hadn't discussed it yet, but it was obvious. It didn't make any sense for us to be living apart and paying rent for two places while we were trying to raise a child.

And whatever. Dean could keep this shit hole for all I cared. He could keep the black lights and black light novelty posters. The Pantera posters. The Slayer posters. The bongs. The dragon skulls. The shop class swords. His ratty couch. He was just going to get evicted anyways.

I didn't care, I just didn't want that sleazy shit, that dangerous pedophile, anywhere near our child. I swear to god he's a for real dangerous pedophile, that sick fuck.


## Telephone Seven


There are a lot of stupid baby names. Like *a lot* of stupid baby names.

Violet, Scarlett, Ruby, Adelaide, Isla, Ava, Harper, Amelia, Seraphina, Imogen, Asher, Caleb, Milo, Hudson, Liam, Oliver, Levi, Jasper, Atticus, Kai and Finn.

These are all shitty, these are all common. Like finding a Li at the dog meat stand. These are the new Johns and Janes. Last year's Ethans and Emmas. When they go to school, they're going to get garbage nicknames. It's true. Or a last name initial added to their name because there's going to be like a dozen of them in their class. Just wait and see.

Place names like Brooklyn, Madison, Bronx, and India suck. And last names that are used as first names make me sick. Cullen, Carter, Cohen, Hayden, Miller, Conner, Grayson, Aiden. They're all garbage. It's a joke.

These parents are sheep. They're stupid. They like think that if they give their baby a unique name, it will somehow make their baby unique. They're wrong. Their stupid average baby will grow into a stupid average adult. It's true. It doesn't matter if they name their dumb baby Rama-Lilac or Penelope-Rose. You can name a piece of shit after any flower you want, but it's still going to stink like shit.

And Celebrities are no better.

Audio Science, Kal El, Moonblood, Pilot Inspektor, Acrobat, Aleph, Kingsley, Kyd, Bear Blu, Spike, Destry.

It's like they let some retard who runs around in a Batman cape name their kid, only they didn't. I swear to god they're wife beaters. Break their bitch's arm. I mean, there's no way you get both parents to agree that those names are a good idea. But really, it's probably just drugs.

Naming your baby after your parents is fine if you love your parents. But then it's like, which parent do you name it after? Because one side of the family's going to feel left out. So that's usually a garbage idea, unless the parent is dead. That way the alive parents look like douches if they get jealous or upset. They can wait until they're dead too.

You can also name the child after a dead pet if you loved your pet and it had a nice name. But not if your pit bull was named Gucci or Diesel or some shit. Naming it after a live pet or a relative's pet is just stupid and confusing because they'll like both look if you call them.

Grandparents are just a shitty idea because they have old ugly names. And it's like trendy to name your kids old ugly names now anyways. Alice, Mavis, Maude, and Matilda will be forgetting their grandkids seventy years from now like the ones that are shitting in their Depends and dying today.

Anybody who names their kids after themselves is crazy. Like egotistical. They need to be brought back down to earth, like to get over themselves. Get publicly gang raped and beaten, like in prison or some shit. I mean, that guy in North Korea didn't even name his kids after himself, and it's like law over there to have his portrait hanging in your bedroom over the bed. Like on your lunch kit and shit.

And some people just get desperate for names, and come up with these weird ones that don't even exist. Or they're just cruel, and they'll call their kids shit like Hitler, @, Satan, IKEA, 4Real, Anus, or long ones that I can't even pronounce. I'm not even making these up, it's like the Government has to throw the parents in jail to stop them.

And if they needed help thinking of a name, there's like no end to the help online. Cool names, cute names, best names, elf names, goth names, hip hop, mythical, odd names, sci-fi, Wiccan, popular, top names, trendy, super hot, unique names... all for real. And there's a hundred other categories.

So I ask Boo what names he likes. He likes Hunter—Hunter Shiloh, Hunter Knox, Hunter Rhapsody, Hunter

Keegan, Hunter Coogan, Hunter Seven. Hunter Mason... Hunter is good for a boy or a girl, he says. And he has a few other names. Brody, Xander, Xax, Kes, Blaze, Bailey, Blaze Bailey, and JD. We're not using any of his names, but I don't tell him that. He'd get thrown in jail or fined if he tried those in Scandinavia or China. I just nod my head and smile.

I throw out a few boy names for him, but I already know it's going to be a girl. I tell him Mikel, Jaxon, Owen, Luc, Heath, Richard. Just some dead people off the top of my head. I don't give a shit about these names and I know we aren't using them. I mean, I don't want to sound insane, but I already know it's going to be a girl. I focused, I asked the universe, I put it out there, I felt it in my bones, and I let it go. This is the Secret to getting what you desire, to manifesting your destiny, and it has always worked for me. Always.

I like the names of the people who spam me. Maybe they're like pretend names, but these are important sounding names. Dynamic. Classy. Interesting. International. Like they're rich. Like old money. Opulent. Like maybe they go to Monaco for holidays, play baccarat and shit, and they want to give me like forty million dollars if I help them transfer their vast fortunes.

Names like Rigoberto Wills, who wants me to know that a thyroid level normalizer is waiting for me, or like Cherin Panayotou, Concetta Peirson, Veronike Joujoute and Mrs. Grace Yee, who says *try scuba diving into her sweet juicy pussy with Our Pills.* Clarissa Montclaire sounds like a French angel.

And they sound like even though they are wealthy and influential and better than us, they like never lost their connection to the common people. They sound like Nelson Mandela. Barack Obama. Desmond Tutu. Amo Bishop Roden. I like these names. They sound like people who only want to help. And Oprah Winfrey, of course. I'm seriously thinking of naming the baby Pharo after her. If I ever have two kids, one of them's definitely going to be named Pharo—boy or girl.

I have always wanted to name my baby Seven. Like even before *Seinfeld*. And now that the Beckhams confirmed it was a good name, I for sure was going to use it. And Boo likes it too. It's ok to name your children after like presidents, world leaders and royalty. And the Beckhams are close enough to being royalty. Even if names like Brooklyn and Bronx and Harper are shit and stupid, it's ok to use those names if you're naming your kid after theirs.

But I already had my name. I knew my baby's name, like since I was a girl.

Telephone.

Her teachers would pronounce it wrong—like on her first day of school. But it would be ok after that. And they would smile and shake their heads and think, *what a smart, pretty name—Telephone—why hasn't anyone else thought of that before? Why didn't I think of that before?...Her parents must be artists, like bohemians or some shit.* I mean, it's like who doesn't love their phone, right? But Telephone doesn't sound like telephone—it looks like it—but it sounds the way the Greek girls say their names. Like Persephone. Or like it rhymes with Stephanie. Like Stephanie-Telephone.

I liked the shortened versions of it too. Like Tel, Tellie, or Fawn. I don't like Fanny. Nobody better call her Fanny. Annie I don't mind so much but it reminds me of this cunt Annie that I can't fucking stand so that doesn't really work for me either. Those are a stretch anyways. Tel, Tellie or Fawn are just fine. Even Sev or Sevie, if it makes her more popular with the kids.

But Telephone Seven sounds perfect.

But really, whatever. I don't give a shit. She can call herself anything she fucking wants when she turns eighteen.

# There was shit everywhere

I didn't expect anyone to be home. Dean was supposed to be like returning empties or waiting in line at the soup kitchen. And Robert was supposed to be at work for another couple hours. But there he was, sitting on Dean's couch with a pile of beer cans in front of him like he was working on a pyramid. He was watching *Days of Our Lives*, and his eyes were all red.

I know Robert's sensitive, but I'd never seen him cry.

So I was all like, Boo... what are you doing home so early? Like all surprised and cheery, like I'm happy to see him. Only really I'm confused. And he keeps watching tv and drinking beer and is all like, I got fired. Or quit. Fuck, I dunno. What are you doing here?

So I was like, I uh... I... the door was unlocked, I knocked and I uh, and... oh my god, Robert... did you just say you quit? Did you quit? Did you get fired? Oh my god. Holy shit... Tell me what happened... what the hell happened?

There was shit everywhere, he said. That's why he quit. There was shit everywhere. It was like shit Viet Nam. Shit everywhere except in the toilet. The animal knew how to flush. It was like rooster-tailed all over the walls. It was on the ceiling, it was on the floor. It was in the urinals. And the reek. The reek of fresh crap. The old smelly bastard had taken off his underwear, whipped it around, and then plugged up the toilet with it. Boo didn't know one person could shit so much.

And I didn't really know what the hell he was talking about, all this shit talk. But I was like so full of sympathy, and was all like, Oh my god, why? Who would do such a thing? What kind of animal monster pig would do this to you, Robert? Why?

So he tells me the story. He says that Elmer, his boss, goes for his afternoon shit. And when he gets out he's all like serious, like all pale. Boo says he looks like he's about to tell them that the family dog has to be put down. Only he says that there's a mess, a bad mess in the shitter, and that one of those doomers better get in there and clean it up.

Robert already knew. And so did Jase. They just played dumb. It was like that for half the morning. Some fat old guy who looked like no stranger to the plunger came in. Like all in a panic, sweating and grunting, needed to use the rest room. A couple minutes later, he left all casual. Jase found the mess when he took a piss, and they were just waiting and hoping for the guys on the next shift to get stuck with it.

So Jase runs out to help some customer that just pulled into full serve. And this is like the first time that Robert's ever seen him do this. He tells me that Jase is the laziest sack of shit. Complete dogfucker. That he's always like, Oh Robbie, my back's sore today, I think I fucked it up yesterday. Me and Dougie were curling that bucket of naphtha in the corner. I did it thirty-six times, he only did it twenty-three. Do you mind getting full serve and I'll get the till? I promise I'll make it up to you tomorrow...

And he'll sit there lazy all day and lean and steal and shove sandwiches and chocolate bars and chips into his moustache until some hottie pulls up. And then he can run out to help. Like a Jesus miracle his back's suddenly ok. And he'll come back in and use the same line he always uses—that she asked for a fill, or that she needed him to fill her up. What a douche.

Robert says that Jase runs out of there like Sasha Grey just pulled into full serve driving the Bang Bus, and it's just Elmer and him and a hose and squeegee. So poor Boo tells Elmer, I am not going to do this. I can't do it. I'll barf, I'll puke. And Elmer says that one of them had better do it, because he's got like a pile of twelve applications on his desk. Twelve guys that would be more than happy to do it. And Jase is done with his car, and he's hiding behind a pump. Peaking. Waiting. Pretending like he's doing something.

The three of them weren't budging. It was like a real Mexican standoff. The Goo Goo Dolls, *Iris*, was on the radio.

So finally Robert like snaps, and says, Fine. Fuck you, I quit. I can't do that. And he like rips off his Jiffy Gas shirt and throws it on the counter at Elmer—Here, use this. And he's like walking out and says, And I know you wear a toupee.

And that was it. He quit. What a horrible day, I tell him. And I like assure him that he did the right thing. That everything happens for a reason. And if it wasn't meant to be, then it wasn't meant to be. And then I tell him not to worry, that there's plenty of gas stations out there.


# elBulli


I dreamed a terrible dream. Fuck I had a nasty dream. It was like deep sleep, so I was lucky to wake up without having a jammer. Seriously, I thought I was going to die it was a horrible dream.

And I don't think I'm like psychic, but maybe this dream was about twenty-five percent psychic. It was so deep and vivid, it was like for real.

I was sitting on a seawall, with my friend Amy from college. It was like this path in a Mediterranean painting by the sea. It's the late afternoon, summer. I can smell the tide and taste the Campari, like Negronis or some shit—it's so real. And we're having this awesome conversation. Amy's like, When I get up in the morning, and meditate, and do yoga... it's... it's just like... *awesome.*

And it turns out that we're like in Italy, waiting in line at elBulli restaurant, only there's no people in line, we're just waiting to get in. ElBulli has a waiting list of like a hundred years, but I got this like fancy gilded invitation from Mr. Petrus Cheong.

It's a beautiful day on the seawall. There are families with balloons and berets, tanned young tourists eating gelato, and trained goats that are doing tricks. Everyone's happy. And me and Amy are like having the best time. And then we get a tap on the shoulder, and I can smell Green Irish Tweed. And when I turn my head, it's like I can't believe it, it's like I'm dreaming—it's George Clooney.

Amy is like Ooooh muh gaawWWW!!! Oh muh gaawWWW!!! like she's star struck. And I can't even say anything. I can't believe this is for real. Only it makes perfect sense, with George spending so much time in Italy and all. And I'm thinking this must be a dream... this must be a dream... but he assures me that it's not.

And then George reveals his big secret. He pulls a card out of thin air, like magic, from behind Amy's ear. She squeals. And then he kind of like tilts it, and it's like one of those Cracker Jack holograms. The letters rearrange, and it turns out Mr. Petrus Cheong is like an anagram for George Clooney. He's the mysterious Mr. Petrus Cheong. He tells me that he's been waiting a long time to meet me. That he likes my ideas.

So we're at the door. It's like this beautiful old red wooden door with green and gold detail that's like built into the side of the cliff, and you can barely tell the bricks from the rocks and ivy. I don't know if this is what elBulli really looks like, but it did in my dream.

Some midget with one of those like masquerade masks seats us. And the kitchen sends us all this food that doesn't look like food but you can eat it. And it's all like gorgeous and delicious and I wish I could like remember some of it so I could make it. George tells us that the real reason he brought us here is because he's looking to settle down. Because he's like, you know—a real guy, and has a hard time meeting real women. We're having the best time. A perfect time. And then I feel like I have to take a shit.

So I like excuse myself and I feel like I'm losing control of everything, and I go to the shitter. It looks like a Swedish sauna or spa or something, and the details are getting darker and sketchy. A lady offers me some fondue, which I take, and then I go to like some corner. And I'm sitting, and I think I'm like taking a shit, only I'm accidentally shitting birth to my baby. And I'm like, Oh my god, somebody help me, I'm giving birth.

So the staff start helping me and they clear the shitter, which turns out to be the kitchen—like I was shitting and giving birth in the kitchen. Only they don't have all their medical equipment, so the chef does the best that he can. And he's like intense, and he's pumping my gut like I'm having a jammer, and he keeps going push, push, push! And then George comes in and wants to see me, like is everything ok? And I'm like so embarrassed.

And then I give birth. Only there's like problems. The baby is retarded. It's an ugly retarded looking baby, and hairy like a monkey. And my heart sinks. I feel like we should try this again. Is there anything I can do? I'm so upset and confused, I want to like sue the kitchen or something. They tell me that the best thing I can do is breastfeed. To feed it only organic local bananas, and that I have to like put on this fake boob harness so that it can like suck the banana mush out. The chef says that if I keep doing this—and it may take a couple of hours or a couple of years—that there is a chance that the baby could turn normal. Only I can't do it back here because it's against restaurant policy. Then the chef named it

Corky—like it's the rules of his kitchen he says—and had me sign the papers.

So I go back out, and sit with George and Amy. And I'm breast feeding my retarded baby and it's like trying to eat the food on the table, and I'm like smacking it, going, No, baby! No! Drink! It's for your own good! And I'm trying to be all casual, and I'm like, Can you believe that they will not allow me to breast feed my baby in this restaurant? Like it'll kill someone to see my boob? I thought this place was supposed to be like all progressive and cool? And then Amy's all like, Oh muh gaw... *that's* your baby??? You have like a retarded baby??? For real??? Oh muh gaw... you're always bragging about your baby... *that's* your baby? LoL?

And I tell her, No, of course it's not my kid... I'm like babysitting. Then the baby goes Eeeeeewww-woooooooo!!! like real loud. Like so loud that everybody can hear. And then it turns into this retard that's sitting in a wheelchair, like a retarded boy. But he's got pink barrettes in his messy hair, and there's like this string of green snot dripping six inches from his nose, and he like sucks it all back into his nostril. Eeeeeewwwwwooo!!!

And then George laughs and gets in close with Amy, touches the bottom of her back, and whispers some shit about my retard, and the weird loud whooping noises it's making. How people should have a little more respect for other patrons before bringing their retards to restaurants. And then he says to her that he's had enough, he's lost his appetite. That he's getting fucking sick, that he feels like puking. Doesn't like all the drool and the smell.

Eeeeewwwwwoooooooo!!! my baby goes, and they're both like trying to hold in their laughter, but they can't, and they burst out laughing and run away holding hands.

And then I know that I can't do this. I can't have a retarded baby. This is so not fair. It's not right. It's just nasty. So I like look in my purse and I have no money to pay for the delivery or food. All I got is this hairy baby in my handbag. I tell the waiter that I've got to go to the shitter.

And I think that what I did next was out of compassion. It can be a hard, shitty world for those who are different. I filled up the sink with water and I stuck the baby's head into it. A couple of the nurse-waiters came in to wash some vegetables, like leafy greens, and ask me if everything's ok? Will I be long? And I'm like, Oh ya, I'm just washing my hands. They say they'll use the other sink, and leave.

I figure after a couple of minutes the baby should be dead. Only I pull it out and it just kind of goes Eeeeewwoooooo!!! It's not dead, and now it looks like I've beaten it. Like its teeth are all broken, and it's got like a bloody nose and black swollen eyes. So I stick it back into the water, which sort of looks like dirty-red-jello-roast-beef dish water or some shit, and it's filled with glass and nails.

And then its body turns into like a giant bug. Like centipede legs are grabbing and pinching and tightening on my arm and it's trying to get out of the water. So I like freak out. I hate bugs. And I like start smashing it into the sink, against the wall, and it's like digging into my arm more. I smash it into the mirror and grab a shard of the busted glass and start stabbing it and cutting it into pieces. It's kind of like hollow, and yellow stuff is coming out. Even then it's not really dead, it's still twitching.

And then I half woke up, I guess, and rolled over and had a better dream. That I'd like won a trip and a new car on *The Price is Right*. That me and Amy went to Hawaii or Tahiti or some shit and the Brady Bunch were staying next door at our hotel.

# PND.cøm is gay

This morning I ate half a pack of bacon, eight pork sausages, a steak and four eggs, a pile of hash browns, six slices of toast with butter, and a croissant filled with whipped cream and maple syrup—like real maple syrup. And a pot of coffee. I was up early and had plenty of time to make breakfast. Otherwise I make this killer breakfast sandwich with bacon and eggs—like the kinds you can nuke—and ham and cheese in between layers of Eggo waffles. It's so fucking good and so fast to make that sometimes I even have it as a snack. I mean, I'm eating for two now.

And it's like, I'm a spiritual person, but I'm not religious. I had to make sacrifices for my family now, even if it meant becoming a fat fucking pig. It's not like I wanted to get fat, except I had to. But I'm not like one of those Catholics or shit that was going to feel guilty about it. Guilty's for fucking losers. Guilty's for the idiot who goes to jail to suck cock and get raped in the ass. If I had to be a fattie, I was going to enjoy it. Like live in the moment, live in the now. Like Eckhart Tolle. I don't ever waste a day of my life feeling guilty.

But it's not like I'm an inconsiderate cunt. I have this account on pregnationdivas.com—yummymummy69. I originally wanted yogamom69, but it was already taken, so whatever. Anyways, I started a thread.

YUMMYMUMMY69: i am 12—14 weeks pregnant. when is the best time to tell others that i'm pregnant? like work specifically? thanks    ; )

CALIFORNIACOUGAR: I told everyone right after I found out. Right away! It was such a surprise! And I was just so excited and I can't keep a secret, lol! But whatever feels right for you!

JULIE23: Pregnancy is a time for support, for community. I also told everyone when I found out. You shouldn't feel like you need to hide it. That being said, a lot of women feel more comfortable to wait, in case of miscarriage.

YOGAMOM78: Personally, I want my power circle and community involved in all aspects of my child bearing time, good or bad. If my baby does not emerge from her dreamtime, I want all the support and love I'll need to move on and heal and grow. Blessings.

YUMMYMUMMY69: i'm not like worried about m/c. i mean, i had to abort twice once, they couldn't get it all out, lol    ; P
but I mean, like etiquette, is there like a law or sh*t for when to tell my bosses?

LULULEMOMMA: I'm waiting. I'm VERY superstitious. I think you're OK waiting until your second trimester. For myself, I'm thinking about six months in. I mc'd five months in last time.

RUBMYSWEETBELLY: i here that when you can here baby's heartbeat, baby will not m/c anymore. wait for heartbeat if your worried. xoxo

LOTUSDREAMER: I have had three miscarriages. But with a holistic approach and natural supplementation, I have had three successful pregnancies since. I have a lot of information on this topic on my blog, LotussDreemer@blogghubb.com. Please feel free to visit and "like" me on Assbook.

TRISTANANDKRISTENSMOMMY: i lost my first at 15 weeks. wait as long as you're comfortable. don't feel stressed or pressured. i will pray for you, sweetie. god bless.

RHIANNON29: DON'T!!! DON'T TELL YOUR BOSSES!!! I WAS FIRED SHORTLY AFTER I DID. I DID NOTHING WRONG, I WAS A GOOD WORKER. I WANT TO SUE BUT I NEED TO GET A GOOD LAWYER WHO THINKS I HAVE A GOOD CASE.

HORSEBREEDINGBREEDER: I've had four children and six miscarriages in the last eight years... I've been a busy gal, LOL! But seriously, you get used to miscarriage after a while. It's no big deal, especially after three abortions. You just got to try again. You know... just keep throwing sh!t against the wall and see what sticks! My friends are surprised when I'm NOT pregnant, LOL! Number five on the way... so far, so good! You go girl!

HOTBABYMOMMA82: No Yummy, there are no laws. Rule of thumb is after the first trimester—and people will probably start to notice around then irregardless. You might as well put it out there before they start speculating or asking. Good luck!

LOTUSDREAMER: horsebreeder=troll... you are on

ignore.

CONCETTA_FERNANDEZ: i'm waiting until the doctor feels the baby is safe.... i have had seven miscarriages and it is too painful to listen to all the sympathetic comments.... being reminded all the time, despite everyone's good intentions.... it is just too hard.

Oh my god, not hotbabymomma82. It was time to kill this thread. She is such a fucking know-it-all, especially after having her kid a few weeks ago. Now she's the fucking expert on everything about pregnancy and motherhood.

And her baby's a fucking goof. Seriously. It's like one of those depressed babies that cry all the time. A colic baby. But this bitch thinks the thing's a fucking angel. A little miracle. She brags about it nonstop. Like if it shits it just painted that Georgia O'Keefe vagina, or invented Assbook or some shit. Seriously, it's like the dumbest baby with all it crying and health problems. And ugly. She posted like a hundred pictures. It's got like a weird crooked head. I would shake that fucking baby if it were mine. I definitely wouldn't be bragging about it.

These miserable bitches were a drag. All their miscarriages and shit. I couldn't get a straight answer out of one of them. So I just told my bosses after I logged off. Pregnationdivas.com is fucking gay.

# The Snail and Rooster

I drink every day. Like I don't get shitfaced every day, but I've got to have a drink or two. Like a glass of wine or a bottle to unwind. Like a night cap. It's no big deal, it's like cosmopolitan, like what the European bitches do.

Drinking at home every night gets boring though. Sometimes I've got to get out, or else I've got to take more pills.

But like where to drink? I couldn't go anywhere nearby. Too risky. Everybody at work knew that I was having a baby, and everybody at work is alcoholic. It's true. Like they drink to manage their mental illness or to forget what losers they are, but whatever. Somebody would see me for sure. I couldn't go to any of my regular spots. It's not like I was going to hang out and drink coffee and watch all the fucking drunks act like idiots. I'd need a drink just to cope. There's nothing more miserable than being sober at the bar.

And I didn't want to drive too far out of the way. You get caught driving back and it's just not worth it. DUIs are a bullshit nightmare. I wasn't going to just stay somewhere overnight or sleep in my fucking car.

So it hit me. I would go to a gay bar.

But really I got the idea when I accidentally went into a gay bar. The Brass Horn. I was just popping in for off sales. And I thought it was going to be a sort of country and western bar, but it was like a dirty gay dive bar. Like where dirty hairy gay bears and dirty hairy gay bikers hanged out. Like a bunch of no good dangerous pervs up to no good. Looking to get drunk, looking to get drugs. Looking to get sweaty, looking to get cock. Like horny, intense men. It was just too macho. This was not my gay. I felt like Simon Adibisi and his beany cap would jump out of a booth and stab me. Adibisi with his wild nigger eyes. His big smile, all white and crazy.

I left through a dark hallway with my bottle of vodka. A couple of toughs were necking and grabbing their balls through tight jeans by a vandalized payphone.

But even though the Brass Horn was like gross and full of AIDS and danger, it still gave me the gay bar idea, which was perfect. I didn't know any like for sure gay people, so I wouldn't run into anyone I knew. And I didn't want to hang out with a bunch of dykes, I wanted to hang out with gay men. I once had a lesbian who looked like Leonardo DiCaprio come up to me in bar and say that she liked big girls. Whispered that she had a trough of lasagna back at her place—how would I like to go home with her and eat it? I just didn't need that kind of pressure.

No, I wanted man friends. Gay man friends. Things were getting complicated in my life. Like I had to make a lot of decisions and shit. Like I was making a lot of stupid decisions. And I felt that I needed a gay best friend, like a GBF, to listen to my problems and give me advice.

So I found the Snail and Rooster. It seemed like a normal pub. Laid back, casual. You know, kind of English style—all brass and green and red and dark wood. Pool tables, dart boards. There was like maybe two other women in there. It was perfect.

At first I felt like Holger, the foreign exchange student

with the ponytail. I sat by myself in a booth and pretended to read. I had a couple of martinis and a few sweaty monkeys. That kind of relaxed me and I wandered around a bit, looking for my new friend.

I saw him sitting in a dark corner. A private nook. I could tell he was smart. He was like just sitting there, wearing glasses and drawing zigzags on a keno ticket. He didn't look too gay. I sat down and introduced myself. Started shooting the shit for a few minutes. Like, it was my first time here... nice place... come here often?... the menu looks pretty good... what did he do for a living?

And I'm like doing all the talking and he hasn't said much—I didn't even get his name—and then he tells me that he's expecting someone. It's kind of private, kind of serious, he says. Like one of their best gay friends just died and they had to plan a funeral or some shit. And so that if I really didn't mind, he wasn't so much into socializing, thanks.

It was getting late anyways. I didn't want to be up all night talking to some gay nerd about beauty products. About *Project Runway* and lubricants and anal sex. So I tell him that I have to go, that I hope his funeral works out ok and shit, and that it was nice meeting him.

And I was like heading out and I saw some posters on the wall. One had this dude pulling up his shirt to show his abs. And he's winking and he's got his mouth open, like all fierce. It says *Hard Candy* on the bottom of it. That was coming in a couple of weeks. And there was live music and DJs every weekend. Maybe I'd try then, I figured. It was only like Wednesday. Nothing going on in the middle of the week. So I grabbed a bottle of vodka from the bar and headed to the rear exit near the pool tables. I could always use more vodka.

And I don't know, maybe it was like my paranoia, maybe it was something they put in those sweaty monkeys, or maybe it was like actually for real. I couldn't say for sure—I panicked and left so fast. But it was like he was following me around, like he was some kind of bad karma spy. Like he was trying to ruin my life. I saw him standing behind some dude bent over the table. He was chalking a pool cue, laughing his gross annoying laugh. I swear to god it was him. I swear to god it was Dean.

## C-section

I have a perfect pussy. It's true. I've been told so on more than one occasion.

Boo used to tell me all the time when we started dating. He'd lick my pussy and he'd go Mmmmm... you got a perfect pussy.

Same with my Uncle Randy. I'm not sure if he was like my real uncle or not. I think maybe he was like my half-blood uncle or some shit. I don't know, but I've known him since I was a little girl.

He was in town visiting mom. She was at work, and we were drinking and playing cards. I was fifteen, it was hot and the end of summer, and I was beating Uncle Randy at poker.

And I think I won, but I don't know, I really didn't know what I was doing at the time.

So I was all drunk and excited. I clapped my hands, snapped my fingers, tilted my head to the side and was all like, Woooooooo! And then I like dragged the poker chips to my tits. I think I started bouncing and dancing in my chair, and really maybe it was all too much for Uncle Randy.

He just reached across the table, grabbed me by my throat, and smacked me in the face. I was like stunned. Then he pulled me by my side pigtail onto the floor, onto the cards and poker chips, and he had sex with me. I mean, I don't think he really raped me, but there's probably some sort of laws against underage incest.

And that's pretty much how we spent the rest of our time that week, until mom caught us with Uncle Randy's dick halfway down my throat. And that was the last time that I ever saw Uncle Randy. But I was like still reminded of him going, Mmmmmmmm...... you got a perfect pussy, whenever Boo said it.

And you know what? I've got to agree with them. There's a lot of ugly pussies out there. Like *a lot* of ugly pussies. Nasty snatches. And the thing is, mine's all natural. It's not like I've got to work at it. A lot of girls will put all sorts of weird ointments and shit down there, or even get surgery. Because they've got like horsepussies. Or labias that hang down to their knees. Or their fat cunt has so many lips and folds that it looks like a Shar Pei. Or they've got a clit the size of a Chicken McNugget. It's true—I've seen them all. And some girls have just got these nasty smelly pussies. Like they've got these diseases. I'm not even going to get started with the diseases.

And then there's the girls in Africa. Like the girls who circumcise themselves. Like hack off their clits with sharp rocks. Their pussies look gross. And then they like die of infection. But whatever. I'm not one to judge other cultures and religious beliefs. They do crazier shit down there anyways, like chop up albino babies in their cribs at night for good luck parts.

But for real, about the only thing I do is like Kegel exercises sometimes. That's it. No special soaps, douches or lotions. And I'm not so much into the waxing if I don't have to. I like to keep a bit of hair down there so that I look like a woman. Like a Phil Collins airstrip, or sometimes a lightning bolt.

So there's absolutely no way I'm letting some baby beat the shit out of my box. It's not worth it. No baby's wrecking my pussy. When I give birth I'll be knocked out and the baby will get pulled out of the hole the doctor makes. It's no big deal. It's just another medical procedure. I've been learning all about it online.

A lot of these silly bitches will go on about their natural births, their underwater births, their standing births, their homebirths, their midwives. Their holistic approach. No epidural. Like they're bragging. Like you'll have an ugly baby, a shitty baby, if you go to the hospital.

Whatever. Any animal—any third world twelve year old—can have a baby the natural way. Any dumb bitch can give birth. It happens a million times a day. It's no big deal. And honestly, it's pretty fucking ugly. Nobody watches a calf fall out of a cow's asshole, all covered in like blood and afterbirth, and thinks it's beautiful. Nobody thinks it's cute after the cord is gnawed off. When the mother and calf eat the shit and blood and placenta, and the calf's lying there all helpless and half retarded. And there's nothing beautiful about some moaning bitch shitting the bed, spraying nasty fluids, while some slimy red fetus twists and drops out of her sweaty hole. Shrieking into the world.

Those bitches can keep their saggy cunts and natural child birth. They can brag all they want. I'm becoming an expert on C-section. I bet that with enough drugs and alcohol and a box cutter, I could do it on myself.


# Egg

I started carrying an egg to work. I even drew a little face on it. It looks pretty good, like a baby.

I once saw this show on the tv where like the kids who go to this school are given eggs. Like to teach responsibility. To see if they were responsible enough to become parents. I always wanted to try that, not because I wanted kids, but because it looked like fun. And I would be partnered up with whichever crush I had at the time, and we would like bond and fall in love. Fall in love while we cared for our egg. Only they never did that at my high school.

I named my egg Hunter. Hunter Shiloh. That's the only time I was going to name my baby Hunter for Robert.

Mostly Hunter just stayed in my handbag. Like I'd just keep it open on the floor by my desk, with little baby Hunter lying on the tissue bedding I made for her. Hunter was a good baby, a quiet baby, and mostly she slept. I'd look into my bag, and she'd just be lying there. Like so peaceful. What was she dreaming about? I did a really good job on her face. The detail.

When I went to the shitter, I'd take my handbag with

me. When I needed photocopies, I'd slip little Hunter into my pocket. When I was in the lunchroom, I'd hold her under my jacket, sort of by my boob. Discreet—not obnoxious—so no one would notice or take offence or think that I was a fucking lunatic holding an egg to my tit. I was like one of those Japanese kids. Those Japanese kids with the electronic pets, or pocket babies. Those little devices they have to like feed, change their shitty diapers, take care of when they cry, or else they like die of starvation, or of broken hearts.

And you know what? This was a good idea. For real, it was a good idea. With my mood pills and my baby egg at work, I don't think I stopped smiling once.

But sometime after lunch, my faery tale ended. The spell was broken. I looked into my handbag, hoping to see her serene face—I really did a good job on that face—and she wasn't there. I checked all my drawers, the photocopier, the lunchroom, I checked the Escalade to see if I left her there when I went for a smoke. She was nowhere. I felt the flash of panic that mothers must feel when their child goes missing, like when I can't find my cell phone. And when I got back to my desk, I saw my jacket on the chair, and the dark patch on the pocket. She'd been crushed. I think it happened at the supply room, while I juggled holding a box, some photocopies, and closing the door at the same time. She didn't make it.

And I was all like, *Fuck me! Fucking gross...* I just kept swearing under my breath, so I wouldn't freak anyone out. I was upset. I really liked that jacket. I'd just bought it, and I hoped the egg wouldn't stain it. And I forgot, or maybe I never knew, what you were supposed to do with egg stains. What a stupid fucking idea. It was obvious from the start it would end this way. Why didn't I just buy one of those Japanese things from the dollar store? I mean, an egg is pretty fucking ghetto, really. It's ok for some sexually active ten year old getting AIDS in Africa who doesn't know any better. But that's about it.

I asked if I could go home early. Like I was sick or something, because I was pregnant. Only I really wanted to get that jacket washed as soon as possible so it wouldn't stain. What a waste of time, waste of a nice jacket. Waste of an egg. But at least I learned a few things. That bringing a raw egg anywhere outside of a kitchen is a shitty idea. That I should probably not sleep with my newborn, so I don't like roll over and kill it. That I was actually pretty attentive, like eighty percent attentive maybe. And that I was going to be an awesome mother. That maybe I just had to practice a little more.

Aw shit, I'll just grab another egg and boil it this time. Draw a better face on it. There's like six or eight in the fridge.


# 9 – 1 1


You helping us move?

What a fucking prick. Unbelievable. And I'm thinking What else, Dean? You want me to lift your car while you change your oil? Need a boost? Got a jar of pickles or two that need opening? What a lazy slug. I hated that we breathed the same air. I wanted to hold my breath, or to stop his. Who asks a pregnant woman to help them move? I mean, I was going to help, but I was just sickened, like just disgusted, that he'd asked.

Yep. We'll find a new home for that couch of yours, Deaner.

Oh my god I wanted to puke. I wish I could've taken that back. Deaner? Maybe it was because I was almost over and done with him? Maybe I was like trying to be nicer? Like when someone's going away, or moving or dead, you act like you'll miss them—even though you're glad to see them go? I don't know. But I was like so grossed out, like appalled, that I just called him by one of his nicknames. He *liked* to be called Deaner. And Weed, or Weedman. He told people shit like, *but you can call me Weed*, because his last name sounded a little bit like Weed. What a douche. Thank god I didn't fucking call him Weedman, or seriously, I would start cutting myself again.

And then he's all like, Thanks. Can't be easy carrying shit with that big belly of yours.

He stuns me. I don't care if he's just joking. You just don't say shit like that to people. I wished he would get raped by a farm animal. For real. A violent pig. Get jackhammered by its monster corkscrew. Split in two by its veiny penis. I wished he'd felch that horny pig and die. With all his skilled slurping and ass sucking. Get an excited hoof right to his stupid face. Bleed to death in all the muck and pigshit.

Anyway, Robert and Dean had no choice but to move. Robert hadn't found a job yet, and Dean had no real income. They only had a few days to get out of there. Robert wasn't legally allowed to drive for another two years, and Dean had a couple of shitty cars, but they were both rotting on front lawns somewhere. That meant we were using my Escalade and Tyler's van. Robert didn't have much to move anyways. I wasn't bringing that shit into my home. It was mostly getting rid of his junk, and moving that sick couch into whatever alley Dean wanted to sleep in.

I was still in a really good mood about all of this. I didn't give a shit what Dean said. It was all over now—life with Dean was finally over. So I was all like, It's going to be weird not having you around so much... you'll have to come by and visit though. Especially when we have the baby. I know we're going to need a babysitter.

And then I kind of scrunched my nose and curled up the corners of my lips, like I was doing my best to fake smile, but it probably looked like I'd just sucked off a lemon.

Only things are never that easy for me. I should have known. Shit changes on a dime. And in a few seconds, I was thinking—this is what I get—this is what I get for trying to be nice. This was like some garbage karma for sure. It was like life just kept shitting on me. Dropping these dirty shit bombs on me nonstop. Dean might as well have been riding a camel and hiding a fucking 9-11 jet under his turban. My world just wouldn't stop blowing up and falling to shit.

Oh I'll be around, he says to me, I'll be around plenty. Robbie said you wouldn't mind if I crashed on the couch for a while until I find a new place.

# How the world is

I screamed at him for like two hours straight. I couldn't answer the phone at work the next day I lost my voice. *What the fuck do you think you're doing telling Dean he can stay at MY PLACE?*

Uh-uh. No way. This was not going to happen. This was so not going to happen. And I wasn't going to be the fucking bad guy about it either. Fucking Robert has no spine. He has no balls. He can't just for once sack up and tell his scumball friend to fuck off. I mean, the idiot texted a breakup to me, I should have known.

I was having my doubts. Serious fucking doubts. I don't mind supporting the father of my child but there was no way in fucking hell that I was going to let that pedophile stay at our home. He was not going to take advantage of our generosity. Like put up some internet feed of our baby while he babysat. Like inappropriate shit. Stroke his finger on its belly. Replace the soother with his toe. Spray whip cream on the baby's nipples. Carefully place a shoe in the crib. I don't know. I don't watch that kind of shit.

Things were going to change around here, I told him.

My hooks were in. I could jerk him around however I wanted now. He was stunned. He just sat there taking it. He just sat there like a child, with his head down, listening and taking it.

And he was all like, I don't know, he's my friend. I've known him since high school. He just needed a place to stay.

And then I school him. I fucking tell him how it is. How the world is. How things are going to be from now on. I'm like, Dean *is not* your friend. Dean *was never* your friend. Dean is a loser. He is a fucking *leech* who hangs off your tit and sucks you dry and then laughs about you behind your back. And I don't want that pedophile anywhere near our fucking child.

And Robert interrupts me, says I shouldn't talk about our baby that way, that he doesn't like me swearing and yelling so much. I hiss at him. I tell him that the baby needs a strong male presence, that a negative influence like Dean in the first year would raise its chances of becoming a homosexual or sexual deviant by seventy-eight percent. It would raise its chances of developing some kind of mental illness or childhood disease by like fifty, maybe sixty percent, I wasn't sure.

Do you want to see the magazine? I ask him. It's all there. It's all there and more. The whole fucking twenty-five year study. I'll find it for you.

And I can't stop, I'm all like, Do you want your little queer to torture small animals? Bite his teachers? Shit his pants until he's ten? Put on my makeup and suck dicks after school? It'll happen—You'll see, it'll happen. I swear to fucking god it will happen, Robert. This is like... scientific fact, this is not bullshit. You just wait and see what happens when you let idiots like Dean hang around and confuse our child. Warp his poor mind. No way. Fuck that. I won't let it happen. I won't. I'll take our fucking kid and you'll never know him or find him, if that's what you want. You'll never see him—we'll live in Siberia...

And then I like turn all red and start bawling and cover my face with my hands.

I'm like no psychologist. I've talked to plenty—I know. But I do know people. And I knew I had Robert right where I wanted him. So he's like apologizing. He's sorry. He was just trying to help everyone. He wasn't thinking. Didn't think I would mind so much. Says he'll fix everything. Doesn't want to upset me and the baby. He's sorry, it won't happen again.

And I stop crying as fast as I started and I tell him—I tell him that it's for the best. That when I make a decision from now on, it's what's best for our baby, what's best for our family. Like, for us. And that I don't need all the drama and stress. All the bullshit. That I just want to give us a healthy baby. And that if he did that ever again, I was scared I might like miscarry or some shit. I didn't know what would happen.


## Moving


Hey, you wanna grab the other end?

The couch was huge. Like one of those ratty old monsters that would never fit around a corner. Like they built the room around it. You'd have to like twist it five times, turn it on its end, turn it on its side, and scratch the hell out of every wall to move it anywhere. It for sure wasn't going to fit in the elevator

He could drag it by himself for all I cared. The fucking retard's like moving with two other dudes and he can't wait until they're back from their load? It was the first thing Dean had said to me all day. He must have known I didn't want him moving in with us. Whatever. I didn't give a shit. I liked it better that he kept his stupid mouth shut. Kept his snaggleteeth to himself.

And it was all good. My awesome mood wasn't just the drugs. I was almost done with Dean. Like I'd never see him again. And if I did, I hoped it would be in the news. Like the obituaries. Or maybe some tragic page five story—like his asshole got flesh-eating disease. Like it crawled right up his shit hole from that gross couch. And after a miracle operation and a painful recovery, he winds up as the half boy. The half boy who pushes his assless, legless self around on a skateboard, inspiring some and disgusting others.

Hell, I'd be happy if he'd just trip down the stairs and bust his scrawny neck. Become like a Superman cripple. Shit in his diaper and piss in a colostomy bag for the rest of his life. Become an inspiration.

So I was all like, Ya... Ya I'll help you Dean... which end?


## Alien


*I feel the heat*
*From my shit—*
*My shit*
*In the bowl.*
*Invading*
*My ass*
*Space.*
*Once with—*

I never realized how talented Robert was. I mean, I knew he was artistic and stuff, but I didn't really know just how much until after he moved in and I started looking through all his stuff.

He has like spiral notebooks filled with shit. Drawings. Poetry. Stories. Music. Robert's kind of like a sensitive guy. It's one of the reasons I'm fascinated with him. He never likes to admit it though. He's got his sort of featherweight/lightweight cage fighter image going on. I mean, he doesn't actually fight, but he looks it. And I love UFC which is another reason I'm so fascinated with him.

*There once was a man who when he shit, he shit sideways.*
*He ate too many hamburgers, and the next day it came out so big and dry it hurt and nearly ripped his asshole.*
*Ew Ew Ew! he yelped.*
*Plop!*
*The man flushed. The shit clogged the toilet. Water and piss and shit rose up and kissed his balls.*
*No No No! he screeched and jiggled the flusher.*
*But it was too late. There was water and piss and shit all over the cracked linoleum.*

That one was pretty new. There was a lot of shit
stories. But I liked his writing, and if he ever wrote a
book, I'd want to buy it—I'd want to buy it and read it
even.

And I know that when he was in high school, he played
bass guitar in his Uncle Grant's church band, Cross Country. They were like the house band for The Ministry of
Light: International Alliance of Christ Church. It was one
of those Mega-churches. Only Boo was never really religious. And after he was arrested for possession of mari-
juana, or for trafficking or some shit, his Uncle Grant sat
him down. He sat him down and told him that he had to
make a decision. Was he going to choose Cross Country,
The Ministry of Light: International Alliance of Christ
Church, and accept Jesus Christ into his life as his Lord
and Personal Savior? Or was he going to run around?
Run around and live in sin, with the booze and the drugs,
the girls and parties?

After that he mostly played in like metal or punk
bands. Yoda's Wiener, PigSlit, ChrisTRapeR. He's got this
one cd  here—Eloquent Negro. He plays guitar on it. It's
heavy and you can't really understand the singer.
There's not that many songs, but they're all kind of
gross.

*The Need to Rape*
*Peachgrinder*

*Sewn-shut Anus*
*Sodomy Island*
*Down Syndrome Girlfriend*
*Masticated Penis*
*Bukkake Suicide*

I listened to it a few times. It's not really my music, but it's good, I think. *The Need to Rape* would be catchy if they got someone like, regular, to sing it.

He also has this folder with pencil drawings in it. It's got *Portfolio* written on it and has an application for some tv art school.

There's a picture of a tiger, like sitting on his belly. He's sort of looking off all lazy to the side, like he's happy. Content maybe. Like, I'm a tiger, what are you going to do about it? There's a mangled arm and a half gnawed face in a puddle of blood by his paws. It would make a great T-shirt. And a there's an illustration of Supertank, which looks like a Corvette or Trans Am or some shit—I don't know—but with like tank tracks and lots of guns on it. There's also like a portrait of an important looking Indian, holding a cigarette. The smoke looks so real.


# A million dogs

I didn't mean to hurt him.

I mean, it wasn't my fault that Dean sucked so bad at moving. That he was so shitty at lifting things. That he was so weak. Dean sucked at carrying things. He really did.

Like seriously, he struggled. The doorway was tricky. A bit of pushing and twisting, not so much lifting. But once we got the couch into the hallway, it wasn't so bad. It wasn't that heavy. But Dean weighs like maybe a buck twenty. And he's wheezing and breathing all loud, and he's got like sweat beading on his forehead and dripping down his nose. It's gross. He looked like he was going to have a jammer, and we haven't even gotten to the stairwell yet.

And he's all like, *Christ in fucking hell*, hey... hey—can you slow down a bit? I'm losing my grip... shit... it's digging into my hands... hold up a bit... let me adjust...

And I must've been like rolling my eyes, but I didn't say anything and I probably walked faster. When we got to the stairwell, Dean insisted that we stop for a minute. To like, you know, give me a rest, and so that he can adjust. And I ask him if he wants to switch sides, and suddenly the break's over.

We got down the first flight ok. I was on top and he was at the bottom. He was concerned for me again, and sweating like a hog and wheezing like some old man with one of those oxygen tanks. Hahhhhhh... Hahhhhhh... Hahhhhhh. He sucked at carrying things. He really did. But he was an angel, like a real dear, with all his concern for me.

He only got down maybe two steps on the second flight, I hadn't even moved, and he was all like, Wait, slow down... shit... hang on a sec... wait... wait, for *fucksakes*... stop a sec, let me get a grip...

For real, I couldn't hang onto the couch. Poor Dean. The thing just rolled over him like he was some bug. I think he was dragged underneath it for a bit, I couldn't really tell. When it was all done, the couch had slid into the corner, and Dean rolled into it. He looked all crooked on the stairs. All bent and twisted like he shouldn't be, like he had new extra joints. There was blood all over his face. His mouth was open, and it looked like his chipped teeth had been knocked out. His eyes were rolled up into the back of his head, like he was sleeping. Only he looked dead.

I nearly burst out laughing—I was so close—but I held it back. It was really hard. So I was all like, Dean?... Dean?... You ok?... Dean? He didn't move or blink or twitch. I called 911. There was probably a lawsuit in this for him.

About a week later when he was stabilized, we visited Dean in the hospital. With all his casts and elevated limbs he looked like one of those marionettes, or like he was all wrapped up and caught in some spider's web. We brought him a box of Ritz crackers, Nestlé Quik, black licorice and pickled eggs. I don't think he could eat any of it. Not that I really cared. I got him some kind of stuffed rat or weasel with buck teeth from the gift shop. Maybe like a possum? I don't know, it looked like him. Robert got him some pervy get well card, with like a re-tarded joke and a naked chick in it or some shit.

He couldn't remember what happened. He was on way too much Demerol and morphine. And I couldn't help but think this was the perfect life for Dean. Like being taken care of by others and given free drugs. And I sort of felt like, even though it was totally an accident, I kind of helped do something good.

Dean wanted to know if we could go the pharmacy for him. Get him a heated donut pillow. And a couple of those bracelets—like an ionic bracelet and a magnetic one. He said his nurse was wearing one of them. I volunteered right away—I was so fucking bored—and left him and Robert.

On the way there, the weirdest thing happened. Like the cosmos or kismet or goddess unfolded. It was kind of like a faery tale, like a spell. Like I was carried on a magic carpet. Snake charmed and led by pipes. Or like I was following my magical dog—the dog that I didn't know was magical—to a cave of a million children and a million dogs, like in that story. I mean, I was just kind of wandering around, I didn't know where the hell I was or where I was going, and then like some sort of dream, I wind up in the baby viewing area.

The babies slept. And I watched them. Transfixed. So tiny. So helpless. It was like looking at the puppies or kittens in the window of the pet store. Not quite as cute, but almost. And I was like hypnotized. I'm sure I was smiling. Like I couldn't stop it. Like I couldn't help it. I was filled with like so much joy about my future, like at all the possibilities, at the wide open world and everything good in it.

I'm sure I probably could have looked for hours, but then somebody, I don't know, like a doctor, a nurse, security? asks me something. Like am I a patient? Am I waiting for someone? Which one was mine? I'm not sure, I really didn't hear. But then I glance at him and I'm all like, Oh, sorry, no. I'm just like visiting a friend. Well, my boyfriend's friend. I'm just looking... I'm pregnant myself. I'm just getting excited is all... they're so small and beautiful...

And I'm still looking at the babies and the voice goes

to me, Are you seeing a doctor, a specialist here, *Miss...*?

And I'm kind of caught off guard and I'm all like, Uhhh, Bradshaw..... Carrie Bradshaw. Ya. No.... I mean, not yet. Just like, you know, my family doctor and holistic practitioner right now. But ya, I'm gonna. I'm gonna for sure—soon. Third trimester in like a month.

And the spell's broken and the room is brighter and I can hear the hospital around me and I glance at who I'm talking to. Security. I tell him that I'd better get going. My boyfriend's waiting. And I walk away and look back, once again at the babies, and once again at the security guard who is like writing something into his notepad.

## Perogy Burger

This girl from work, Kameljit Guptha, invited me for lunch today. I don't really know her, but I understand that being pregnant makes me a little more popular around the office. I get it. It's like everybody wants a piece of the pregnant girl. And I don't know, maybe it was like tradition or good karma in India to buy shit for pregnant girls. Like it would make you more fertile, or you wouldn't have a baby girl or some shit.

Anyways, I like free lunch as much as the next bitch. And I figured that if Angie Jolie and Octosulumom could like, find the time to help filthy third world bums and beggars while raising twenty children, the least I could do was make time for lunch.

So Kameljit grabbed me at my desk a bit after noon and drove us to lunch. She has a silver Toyota Corolla.

It's like really nice, new. There was a Kleenex box above the back seat that had like a golden Kleenex box holder over it. I really wanted one, and I asked her where she got it from. She said that she wasn't sure, that her mother had given it to her. I looked around some more, peeked in the glovebox. Nothing unusual.

There was like an air freshener—or maybe it was just a picture—of some blue Indian woman wearing orange, green and gold hanging from the rearview. One hand was up in the air, like she was going *why not?*, and the other hand was up in front of her tits, like she was going *ok*. And she wouldn't take her wild eyes off me. They were intense.

Me and Kameljit talked on the way. We talked about how nice the weather was a couple of times. How we couldn't believe that summer was already over. We talked about work. Like who annoyed me and shit. I told her how much I liked *Slumdog Millionaire*. I actually didn't mind talking to her. I could understand her, like her accent wasn't too bad. And she just nodded and agreed with everything I said. I told her that I liked the music. She tried to tell me the name of it like three times, but I couldn't understand. She said it was very popular right now. Good to dance to.

After a few minutes we pulled into a small parking lot, and she does this like twelve point turn and parks. We are here, she says. I'm looking around at the—I don't know, plaza?—and there's like a bunch of these little businesses with like Persian or Chinese or Indian writing. I can see words like *Travel* and *Insurance* and *Dry Cleaners* in English. The only spot that looks like it serves food is called Delhi Donuts. The faded sign on the corner says Delhi Donuts... Pork Torta Sub... Noodle Soup... Schezuan Fast Food... Best Coffee... Stop the Lies...

And I was like, Uh... no. Uh-uh. I can't. I can't do it. I'm not going to eat here.

I couldn't do it. I couldn't eat there. It was just too ugly. I imagined the ugly food and the ugly people and I didn't want to be any part of that. It looked like the kind of place that Vietnamese or Korean teens would shoot each at after Karaoke. Or get into machete fights in the parking lot. But Kameljit tells me the food is terrific—like the fried chicken, the donuts, the salmon burger. But maybe do not order the potatoed items, she says, whatever the hell that means. Everything except the potatoed items.

I didn't care. I tell her that I don't want to eat their potatoed items, or any of their food. So I give her the directions to Sean White's and tell her to go there. You're going to love it Kameljit, I tell her.

Sean White's is great. Like casual fine dining. There's like a strict hiring policy where they only hire the hot little bitches. And maybe one fat chick that they hide in the sink, so they can't be accused of hiring discrimination or whatever. It's a place where the young people hang out, like where they try to drink if they can't get into the bars. And where older people go—like when they're in denial—and try to act and dress like they're still young. And then there's the old pervs in suits—like the ones who work at the banks and shit. They come in for lunch. And they laugh and talk loud and flash their watches. They stare at the hot ass and make their pervy jokes and then they laugh some more. Nobody likes them.

We got a booth pretty fast. Our waitress looked like Ellen Page and had a feather clipped in her hair. Like one of those hipster chicks. She was pretty, but she'd be prettier with a boob job. Some extensions and little makeup wouldn't kill her either. Then she'd get the tips. Juno handed us our menus and asks if we'd like to start with drinks. I felt like Kameljit was the kind of girl that I could drink in front of without worrying about her telling anyone. So I ordered a Patrón Margarita, only they were out of Patrón, so I got the Cuervo Margarita instead. But really I bet it was just some shit from a tap. But whatever, I didn't care, it was on Kameljit. She ordered an iced tea.

So Kameljit starts asking me shit like, when am I due? Am I excited? Do I know if it's a boy or girl? And I just give her like quick answers, because really I'm more excited about the menu and recommending shit to her—I hadn't been to Sean White's in a while. And I'm like trying to figure out if I want to start with Spicy Orange Thai Salad or the Blackened Cajun Chicken Salad. I ask if she wants to split the Tuna Tataki and the Calamari with chipotle aioli with me, but she says she's not hungry.

So when Juno comes back I order the Blackened Cajun Chicken Salad, and the Tuna on Soft Corn Taco for starters. Kameljit's at least got to try a bite. And I tell Juno that I'm just dying for the Perogy Burger with bacon, cheddar, and caramelized onion sauce—and if could I get the yam fries with chipotle aioli on the side, that'd be great. I decide a pint of Pilsner will go perfect with it. Kameljit gets another iced tea.

After we order, Kameljit asks me more questions. Like about work. Do I enjoy it? Do I want to keep working year after year? Am I financially secure? Have I prepared for my baby's future? I swear to god she's like reading from a scrap of paper, like a script. And I see where this is going. She'd like to partner with me. Add me to her list of associates. If I have some savings—some money that is not being put to proper use perhaps?—she could make me twenty percent, and yes—even fifty percent—in a year. Together we could all make a lot of money. She is affiliated with Sun Money Systems International.

And I just shake my head. The poor girl doesn't stand a chance. She's got a lot to learn. Like a lot to learn. So I tell her that I'm not interested, but thanks anyways. And then I'm all like, Sweetie, let me tell you about making money—you're going about it all the wrong way. And I explain to her *The Secret,* and what she needs to do to manifest her goals and desires into her life. I share the techniques that all the happiest and most successful people in the world use to make their dreams come true. And she's listening but I don't think she's like understanding, so I tell her I'd burn her some cds.

And then she's all like, You mean you pray for it? That's *The Secret?* And I just like laugh and roll my eyes like she's fucking crazy, and I'm like, *No!* You're not *praying* for it... you're asking the universe and letting it go... you're visualizing what you want so that you'll attract its energy and it will manifest itself into your life. Praying is like for... *desperate people.* People with missing dead children, people with cancer. Shit like that. Or sports fans. It just doesn't work. Praying is garbage, I tell her.

So I gave up and quit talking and tried to finish my food before it got all cold. Only I'm really not as hungry as I think, and I'm like only able to eat maybe half my

Perogy Burger. It's so good, but just like way too much. And I mean, the appetizers were pretty small, but I probably should have just gotten one.

Then Juno comes by and I ask her for the check, please. And if she can wrap it all up for me, that would be great. Then I'm all like, Thanks, Juno. And she looks at me all weird and leaves. She brings everything back and I look at the bill quick before I shoot it to Kameljit. I was glad she was paying for all of this. And I hoped that she made all sorts of money with her pyramid scam to cover it all, but I doubted it.

I was like so full and buzzed that I really didn't feel like going back to work. So I called them before we left and I tell them that I'm feeling sick and pregnant, that I don't think I can make it back. Kameljit dropped me off at my Escalade and I drove home. I had the place to myself, so I uncorked a bottle, hit the couch, and checked out some shit on Assbook. Andre's status was *I am love*, and he was going on about how he didn't think *such a beautiful girl could like me back*. What a sad lovesick fool. Some girl was arguing with him about his status.

I passed out on the couch with my open bottle and open laptop. For real, that Perogy Burger just knocked me out.


## Number One Killer


Frona isn't on Assbook. She has this blog that she keeps her travel photos on. Fronablog, I think.

She sent the office a couple of postcards, but mostly

she updates her blog once or twice a week and says hi to everyone on there. Anyways, she hadn't updated in about two or three weeks and we found out through this woman at work, Nancy, that she died.

It was sort of sad, I guess. We were all looking at her blog, like at all the pictures. Seeing how happy and excited she was. Like how much she was enjoying life. There she was with a bunch of old broads on Kilimanjaro or some shit. There was Frona pointing at a giraffe. There she was on one knee, handing a ball to some smiling African kid.

So we all left like these RIPs and goodbyes and sad face emoticons on her comments page.

And it turns out that the number one killer in Africa is not the lion or tiger, it's not the cobra or crocodile—it's the hippopotamus. The hippopotamus maims or kills more people in Africa every year than any other animal. I mean, they look slow and stupid, and they look friendly enough—like you could like walk up to one and feed it a cabbage—but it turns out those things can move. Like faster than people. They'd rip your arm off with that cabbage, they'd rip you in two. Easy. They don't give a shit for people. I mean, they're herbivores—they don't *need* to kill people—they gore or trample people for fun.

So poor Frona was like on some kind of river safari or whatever, and they were watching these monsters from the boat. And I guess she was like leaning over too far, trying to take a picture of the hippos, like maybe to add to her blog, and her handbag falls in the river.

Anyways, you just try finding insulin in some asscrack sweaty jungle in Africa. It doesn't happen. They can't even afford to give kids a one dollar malaria shot. So I guess she went into a coma that day and died before they could get her to the medical tent or elementary school gym in time.


## This is What's Wrong


I got home from work. Robert was watching some shit about toddler beauty pageants. He was drinking and his eyes were red and it looked like he was crying. Seriously, did he just sit around and drink and cry every afternoon? So I was all like, What's wrong, Boo? He wouldn't answer. Or look at me. He was like, Nothing. Nothing's wrong. Don't worry about it.

He stared at the tv. Some blond brat with big hair strutted and smiled on a runway, and then shrieked all red-faced at her trailer park mom backstage. She was having a fit. I wanted to knock out her little chiclets. Shake her by the shoulders, give a couple good slaps to that little whore mouth.

I guess he thought I'd leave him alone to pout, but I kept pressing. Because we're a team. And that's what people in love do for each other, and I wouldn't leave him alone or let it go until I could help him.

So he was like, Fine. You wanna know what's wrong? This... this is what's fucking wrong... And he pulls some papers from the coffee table and throws them at my face. And then he grabs the bologna sandwich from the ashtray and throws that at my face too, but he misses and mustard blows up all over my tits. So I was all like, Fuck off! What the hell's the matter with you? I'm only trying to help, you fucking asshole! And he was like, You want to help? Fine! Read it! Read it, bitch! You said you want to know what's wrong? This... this is what's fucking wrong!... Here! Go ahead, read it... make it all better...

I was like furious. We kind of went on like that for maybe five, ten minutes, and then we calmed down and apologized and everything was better. I looked at the papers to see what he was so upset about.

IN THRALL OF THE LICH KING:
BOOK ONE OF THE
THREE THRONES TRILOGY

*By Brooks Cassiar and Jordan Korso*

PART ONE—CORSAIRS ON THE FRINGE OF TIME

...And Savage Rex
Son of War
Fought on through
th' blood and gore
And would not stop
'til lust was fed
To swing his sword
and slay them dead...

—verse viii, chapter xiv *Calliope of Wyrd*
By Pharnasuss Quailsong, Poet Laureate of the Royal Court of King Toran III, of the Fourth Age

117

The lone elf ran across the blue vastness of the barren moonscape. What had first been a sliver on the horizon now loomed before him an ebon monolith. Just beyond it, he could see the constellation of the Dragon—the tail still within the House of the Heliosphere. This boded well. He still had time for passage through the ephemeral Rook, across space and time, to U'ros below. He was so close.

Only something was not right.

He slowed, and crouched by an outcropping of blue, quartz-like moonstone. His keen, silver eyes scanned the area. The Great Rook—origins lost in the Myst Tyme, one of the Twelve Towers in the Realms of Illeia, and the only one on his home of Elmenaar—was lifeless. Green Mother U'ros rose in the South.

This was a trap.

The tail of the sky Dragon was exiting the House. Once the constellation left the House, the Tower would disappear, would become a mirage lasting three cycles, and no one could enter. Travel through it would be impossible. The Tower began to waver.

The danger mattered not—he had to enter the Rook, or his mission would be lost. The Knight ran purposefully. His crystal armor, like the landscape animated, was but a shimmer to the eye as he stealthily sped to his destination.

He cautiously entered the circle of megaliths, silently drawing his sword. It was pure crystal, like blue ice. It pointed like a compass towards blood, towards the enemy, vibrating in warning. It now anxiously pulled his grip in the direction of the tower.

At the base of the Rook, he saw the fallen guardians. The Keepers—all three, slain. This was not possible. Three of the greatest warriors, selected from the King's Royal Elite. Trained for decades in the harshest conditions, under the lethal eye of the Monks of the Silver Crescent. Eighteenth level Meridian Lifeflow—all Masters of Death. There were few men who had achieved that level, and now three of them lay dead before him. The Keepers were trained to hold an army within the Tower for days. Who could have done this?

A figure emerged like a shadow from the Rook, his black clothing like ragged night. He was blindfolded with a long, black cloth, the ends flowed easily behind him. He had no weapons, and he walked confidently, flexing his fists at his sides. An aura of danger, like ozone, crackled around him. He stopped suddenly, only yards away from the Elven Knight.

The Knight observed the man. He did not know they were real. He had only heard legends of them. They were given many names, in many stories—all fantastic, all frightening, all imposing, and all—at least it seemed now—too real. The Brotherhood of Blood. The Reavers. Perfect Death. The Mage Smashers. They Who Cannot Not Be Killed.

"Are you the One named Elyhol'eheymn, son of Eiyerrekh?" asked the shadow.

"Aye." answered the Blue Knight.

"Then you are in possession of something I require..."

The last star of the Dragon's tail hanged in the House of the Heliosphere.


I could only read the first page of it. I didn't understand any of it, like what the hell it was all about. I'm pretty sure I don't like that kind of shit. It's kind of like garbage. Like shitty and gay. But I was all like, Um, I don't get it... I mean, I don't get why you're upset? This is good. This is like really good. It's, uh... I think it's really good.

And he kind of just leaned his head back on the couch and rolled his eyes. He was looking at the ceiling and just laughed quietly and shook his head, like I was the biggest retard in the world. And then he sucked back the rest of his beer and looked at me, like with disdain, like I was Jacob, the smelly kid in fifth grade. The kid who always wore the same clothes and the dirty red ski jacket that the teacher bought him because he was so poor.

And he was all like, You're right. It is good... It's *real* good. That's the problem. *That's* the fucking problem, man, right there... I didn't write it... Tyler did. Fucking Tyler wrote it. He gave it to me at work... fucking rub it in my face after I showed him the first chapter of my shitty story...

So then I was all like, Well who gives a shit if it's good? And honestly? I don't really like it anyways. Like seriously... it's pretty gay. That poem? Robert, trust me, there is so much wrong with that story... It sucks, really. Your stories are way better than that.

And then he's all like, You just don't understand this shit... it is good... it's really good. I had almost the exact same idea back in high school but he just wrote it better than me. It's like he was reading my mind... the moon... the blue elf... the tower. Fuck, I don't even know why I should even bother. I mean, I'll never...

I wanted to tell him to quit being such a fucking cry-baby. To grow up. But I know he's artistic. Sensitive. And I wanted to support him even though I thought all this shit was retarded. So I took a page from Oprah. You know, take the high road. And I was all like, Well, I'm sorry, but um... you don't have to be condescending... you know? I was only trying to help.

And his voice started cracking like he was about to cry again, and I can tell he's sorry. And he's like, Aw fuck, whatever... I'm sorry, man. Don't worry about it. It's no big deal. I'm just upset. It feels like nothing's working out. I feel like I'm... I dunno.

And then he got up and grabbed the rest of the beer and his jacket. And I think he was more like talking to himself than he was to me, and he was all like, Fuck it. I don't care. It's all fucking gay and a waste of time any-way... Fuck it. Fuck it, man. I'm going out.


## Prana Red Tara—Che Revolution


Oh my god. I just kept saying to him, Robert, you are so going to love this.

The website's beautiful. I looked at it for hours at work today. Real quality. You can tell it's a topnotch product.

On the homepage, there's like hot young people. They're running along some blue beach. Laughing, having fun. It's like paradise. And there's a poem by Rumi on the left. The writing is minimal, stylish, elegant. It blends into the gorgeous photo like art. There's prompts in the bottom right corner, like *Why Prana?, Philosophy, Products, Chillzone,* and *Recall Notice.* And when you open these, there's like pages filled with Kabbalah, Tibetan and Yoga imagery, which I just love and is really so me.

I didn't see any babies, but on this one page, *Let the Right Choice Find You,* there's a picture of those like Buddha toys arranged on a mat, with a little hand hovering over them. Like he's being tested to see if he's the Buddha. And the little hand is sort of hesitating, like over something that kind of looks like a dildo with tassels on it. Horny baby. Little perv.

Anyways, when you select the dildo—or any other item—it goes to this page with a Buddhist prayer wheel. And it kind of like rotates so that you can highlight and select the Mega BTU—the Baby Transfer Unit—that you want to read about. Or you can just fill out the SAT, which is Sanskrit for *pure essence.* It's like a personality quiz. It figures out how active you are and shit to find the perfect Prana to fill your lifestyle needs.

Because I am active, outgoing, gregarious, aware, esoteric, unconventional, fearless—the SAT says Embrace the Fierceness Within, The Prana Red Tara—Che Revolution SR is the pram for you.

If you click on *Inspiration/Essence,* it gives a description of the Red Tara. It says:

In Tibetan Buddhism, Tara is an important deity,

born in primordial time... There are different aspects of the Tara—Red, White, Yellow and Green. *Red Tara*—the Kurukulla, like you, is the fearless, magnifying goddess. A female Buddha. A fierce sexy Bodhisattva. The giver of life, the protector across all of existence and life's oceans. It is no coincidence she is regarded as the goddess of love, sex and magicks... Red Tara—The Magnetic Enchantress, Bewitching Seductress, Consort of Avalokiteswara and sometimes of Vairochana.

And it like goes on about her seven eyes and lotuses on her shoulders and shit, but whatever. You can also click on the Yellow Tara and Green Tara models, but I'm just not into that other Tara shit.

And there's a quick bio of Che Guevara, who I already knew by the picture, but learned was like a rebel. A cool guy with a beret. A guy who didn't go along with the herd. An individual. A communist. Who followed his *own* Truth. Who *owned* his Truth. And in the same spirit as Che Guevara, the buggy blazes an exceptional life path. Even if it is on the outside, on the fringes, difficult, where the timid and the conventional fear to go.

Own Truth.
Extreme Your Serene.
PRANA RED TARA—CHE REVOLUTION SR

And then you click on the purchase information button.

It was weird. Like these people could read my mind. This was so me. I needed this. This was the only option.

This was suited for the active urban spiritual mother—
for the perfect mother—which I was going to be. And it
would really help me shed the pregnancy pounds. There
was no end to the features.

—ARMS OF VISHNU function transmutates the car-
riage into multi-use Pilates equipment for group
workouts in the greenspace. WHEELS OF SHIVA al-
lows the buggy to be towed behind your favorite
two-wheeled ride while you're cruising around the
city.
—Two cup holders—One for mother's chai or cap-
puccino, and the other for energy or protein drink.
No bottle holder for Little Bodhi. We at Prana ad-
vocate and recommend mother's milk for her
mindful, physical, and spiritual nourishment.
—BANYAN WEATHER GUARD—Keep Little Mustard
Seed protected no matter what the conditions.
—TRANSCEND THE TREND with our PASSIONATELY
DETACHED CARRY SLING TECHNOLOGY—Carry Little
Bodhi front or back with confidence, no matter
what the trend, with our easily removable organic
hemp harness. Or add Little Bodhi as resistance
weight to your bicep curls, squat thrusts, lunges,
yoga, Pilates and trail running. Wellness/Babylates
cd and link included with purchase.
—Space-challenged? No need for clutter with our
patented EIGHTFOLD PATH E-Z STOW TECHNOLOGY.
Although we think you will agree—our prams are
sleek and modern and add elegant decor to any living space.

I did some background checking on chat sites, on *Wikipedia,* and *Consumer Reports.*

*Consumer Reports* didn't like their products, and gave it like one or one and half circles mostly. Going on about safety, recalls, flammability tests, shit like that. But I mean, even the most reliable and trusted brands have recalls. They used terms like *Avoid, Poor Quality,* and *Not Recommended.* They didn't care that it came in Bliss Red, Burnt Orange, and Guacamole. Their highest rated one, the Prana White Tara—Teresa Calcutta SR, got two and a half circles. But that's like the basic model.

I didn't care, they just had a hate-on for Prana. Like guilt by association because they used to be Samsara. You don't want to recommend the stroller that kills babies right? Whatever. I just saw some security footage of a geezer plowing his Cadillac into a 7-11 and knocking a Prana through a display of baked beans and into the Slurpee machine. I don't know about the baby, but the buggy looked fine.

*Wikipedia* explained that Prana used to be named Samsara, which had the Hinayana, Mahayana, and Vajrayana models, or respectively, the Narrow, Great, and Diamond Vehicles. Anyways, boring story short, they had to like file for Bankruptcy or Chapter 11 or some shit because some babies died. Some woman was like extreme baby running over a lava flow, like filming some dumb shit for her ghetto fitness blog, and the harness broke. The baby like fell into a hot crack or lava and died. And apparently there were a few kids that got maimed and nearly decapitated when the folding frames collapsed.

There's like some popular and funny YouTube clips. They show these things closing like leghold traps, like cutting watermelons in half. Or chopping dolls that are filled with like fake blood and jello. Some people have just got too much time.

That didn't matter to me. I clicked on Chillzone—the Prana sharing site. I read poetry, saw some tasteful black and white yoga nudes, watched music videos, and checked out some workout routines and organic baby food recipes. All by Prana users. They were pretty good.

*Embrace the fierceness within... Extreme your Serene.*

Like they know exactly who I am. Like they wrote it all about me. Wrote it for me. A new mantra.


## Serious perv


Robert didn't even last a week.

I got home from work and saw him drinking beer on the couch and watching some sports talk show. I don't know what's more boring—watching sports, or watching guys talk about sports. I mean, I've tried watching that shit with Robert, but I just don't get it.

He gets real emotional though. I've seen him throw remotes, beer bottles, and phones against the wall. But if his team wins, he'll be in a great mood for hours. It's like, if the right nigger gets the ball, he'll go Yesss and pump his fists by his head, or go Ya! and pump his fists by his side. Sometimes he'll even jump up and laugh and take a big pull on his beer and smile.

If the wrong nigger gets the ball, or the ref makes a shitty call, he'll be all like, *Awww for fuck's sake,* or *Je—sus Fuck—ing Christ,* or *are you kidding me?... you've got to be fucking kidding me... fuck!* Sometimes he'll look stunned, and throw his hands up and shrug like he's amazed. Or sometimes he'll just smile in disbelief and shake his head in disgust and get up all angry for another beer. Other times he'll bark *fuck!* and smash or punch something and leave.

I didn't need that kind of drama when I sat on a couch. I could care less what a bunch of fucking millionaires did with a ball.

Anyways, I thought he was supposed to be working at the Petromax. Tyler just got him a job there. It was kitty corner across from the Jiffy Gas—that's how he and Tyler new each other. But he says that he got fired. At least he didn't seem too upset. He wasn't crying.

He tells me that his boss, Tony, called him into his office. Needed to talk to him, says it's important. Robert's not sure why. Tony says it's some real serious shit. So Robert's trying to think of how he screwed up. He didn't smash the bay window—he wasn't even working that day. Pete found a bed pan in a customer's car and told Tyler to think fast. Tyler ducked just in time. The official story was neither of them saw what happened—they were both busy somewhere else, but they heard the smash. Maybe it was a drive by? All they could do was sweep up the evidence.

The only thing Robert could think of was a couple of idiots on motorbikes.

The one guy rode a red seventies Honda enduro and looked like a cartoon chipmunk with glasses. Real nice guy, real friendly. And he was one of those guys who always wore shorts. Like cutoff jean shorts, right up until the winter, when he'd vanish. He rode into the Petromax almost every day and would empty his tight pocket of change and get maybe a buck of gas. The first time Robert got him at full serve, Tyler ran off to the shop laughing.

So Robert walks up to him and the chipmunk's like smiling and digs into his pocket and pulls out eighty-five cents. The change was warm. And he goes to Robert, Hey, didn't you work across the street before? I never go there—they cut their gas with water...

And he looks at the embroidered name tag on Robert's grimy jacket and he's all like, Let me introduce myself, Stephan, I'm... and Robert can't remember his name, but the guy sticks his hand out for a handshake. So Robert grabs it and the chipmunk's handshake is limp and pathetic and gross. He just holds his hand out like a prince. And Robert just wants to quit.

And Boo's kind of waiting for him to get off his bike the whole time. Only he doesn't. He sits there and smiles and waits for Robert to unscrew the gas cap and pump the eighty-five cents of gas between his bare legs. Robert sees a piece of ball squeezing out of a rip in the chipmunk's cutoffs, and he like turns his head and undoes the gas cap. The shit people endure for minimum wage. Then he puts the nozzle in the tank and pumps the gas like he's feeding a crocodile or a shark or some other dangerous shit.

But poor Boo was like so flustered that he over pumped, and he like yanks the nozzle out and spills gas all over the chipmunk's pasty leg. Only the chipmunk just laughs and starts his bike and takes off, like that just made his day. So Robert doesn't think he would have complained to Tony.

The other guy was a real douche. Some biker. They're the worst, Robert tells me. They pull up, get off their bikes and stand there with their arms crossed. They don't even talk to you. Maybe they'll just say five bucks, or fill it. And then they'll watch you. Like all intense. Like the serious perv on gyno row—the scary one that's not even smiling. The one that the strippers avoid. They'll watch that you don't spill a drop on their serious custom paint jobs.

Robert spilled a couple drops. But it wasn't even like his fault, he said. It was like the nozzle's connector, like where it swivels on the hose. It had a small leak and it dripped. It landed right on the howling wolf's head, but missed the skull moon. Robert says it was like slow motion, like he knew what was coming next.

The biker shit his pants, started whining like a baby. So Robert gets a squeegee, like hc's going to wipe the tank off. And the biker is all like, What?... Are you fucking retarded? You're going to scratch the paint with that! Fuck! Just fuck off... go inside—go inside and get the manager... I want to talk to the manager.

And it was all just too much for poor Boo, and he snapped. He yells at the biker. He yells at him and tells him to fuck off. I'm the manager! he says, and raises the squeegee like all threatening—like he's going to smash it over the biker's head. And then he swings it at him, like so the birdshit-bugwater sprays onto the biker and his motorbike.

And I guess the biker isn't so tough when he's getting a squeegee waved in his face, and takes off on his loud piece of shit without paying. And Robert kind of chases him, like yelling and shaking his squeegee, Get the fuck off my lot, you asshole! Get the fuck out of here and don't come back, you bitch!

So Robert's sitting in Tony's office, thinking that he's going to get fired over some scuzzy biker, and Tony tells him there was a problem with the float his last couple shifts. It's been short a couple hundred bucks. Does Robert have anything he wants to say? Anything he might know about that?

And Robert knows what's going on. It's Tony's nephew, Adam. He works there and rips off the place so he can buy junk. Everybody knows it. Everybody except Tony. Sells batteries out the back, steals cigarettes, shit like that. He probably just figured it was an easy three-four hundred bucks dipping into the till with the new guy on shift.

So Robert keeps his mouth shut, doesn't want to start trouble. He says he doesn't know what happened. It wasn't him—check the video—he made all his drops. And Tony tells him that it's too bad, he wishes he would have come clean, but he's got to let him go. Says that shit didn't start going missing until he started working there. Doesn't want thieves and liars working for him.

So Robert doesn't like being called a thief or a liar, and tells Tony to go fuck himself. And that maybe he should ask his junkie nephew where the money is. He says that everybody knows Adam is a junkie, that he gives blow-jobs out back for twenty bucks. And he grabs a twenty from his dirty work jacket and throws it at Tony's face, and is all like, Here, why don't you give that to your nephew. And then he stuffed the rest of the money into his own pockets and left.

So I'm like, Well, maybe gas stations aren't for you,

Boo. And I tell him that I think he can do a lot better. Way better. Like with his writing. That I think that he and Tyler should like really maybe try to write a movie. Like a screenplay. With those swords and elfs and whatnot. And I tell him that, even though I don't really understand any of that shit, I do know that we're all like stars, and that none of us should be digging ditches or pumping gas or shovelling pigshit. Especially with a talent like that.


## Milk


I brought Dean some Halloween candy and left Robert there for a visit. Dean seemed upbeat, like he might be in the hospital for a while. He was talking about his back injuries and shit. Like giving letters and numbers to the fractured bones. I don't know. I didn't really understand or give a shit. He was convinced that once he got out, he'd get some decent disability checks, that he wouldn't be like too retarded or gimpy or crippled.

I actually felt good for him, like for real. And I was happy that even though it was like totally an accident, that I kind of helped sign his lottery ticket. This is what Dean had always wished for, and I guess it's what I'd always wished for too. *The Secret* had worked—our dreams had been manifested. Everyone was happy. And I'm not even lying—I was even starting to not mind Dean. It was like the drugs did a good job of slowing him down. Like he was less shifty, less of a rat. Like they made him a normal person. I honestly hoped that the doctors would always prescribe these drugs to him.

But whatever, I took off and checked out the maternity ward.

I said hi to Ken on the way in, and he's like, Hi Ms. Bradshaw. I've been there a few times since my first visit, and Ken's been there every time. Ken is like Hawaiian or Samoan or some shit. A big dude. His name is actually Kahana, but he says Ken's easier to read on a name tag. He's a really nice guy. Like middle aged, with little grandkids of his own. The staff and patients and even the babies like him. He's always happy, always friendly. And why wouldn't he be? working in the maternity ward.

So I've asked him all sorts of questions on my visits. Like, You're security? You protect my baby? Even when you're on lunch? No one can get in? You're sure? And one time I tell him about this hospital in Jamaica. I ask him if he's ever been there, but he hasn't. And I tell him about this crazy bitch who went in and breastfed a baby. She wasn't even like a mother. She just snatched a baby and breastfed it. Breastfed it her AIDS milk. Like for real it happened. I don't know if the baby caught her AIDS or not.

And he points to the cameras, and how nobody can get through the door to the babies unless they have a security card. And that mothers and family and friends can only get buzzed in if they sign in with Bree and Heather at the desk. And he asks me if I see those bracelets and anklets on the babies. They have to match the mother's bracelet—or baby and mother go nowhere. There's all sorts of protocol. Very strictly followed. Carrie, he tells me, Your baby will be in safe hands. You and your baby have nothing to worry about.

I didn't have any questions for Ken today, I just looked at the babies. He was right—the babies were safe. And when it was time to pick up Robert I just smiled and waved goodbye. Bree smiled and waved goodbye too.

Bree, you tan bitch.


## Edward and Bella


I kind of shrieked. Like tears just started pouring out of my eyes. I mean, I was even surprised by my reaction. I think there's something wrong with me. Like for real. I wasn't even faking it.

Robert was all like, It's fucking stupid. It's gay. It doesn't make any sense. Asking me all this bullshit, like *why* is she pregnant? *How* is she pregnant? Why do they glitter? And I don't know. I just don't know. I just wanted us to dress up as Edward and Bella for Halloween. And I mean really, it was no big deal, but for some reason, it was like the end of the world for me. Like we had to do it. And it's not like I'm one of those girls who wears a trench coat and has wet hair and walks around in the rain, but I love *Twilight*. I love it.

But he didn't want to do it. Dress up as a vampire. I think he finally agreed just to calm me down. And he made me promise I wouldn't bother him with any of this dumb shit again next Halloween. I agreed to his emotional blackmail, his Osama terrorism, but whatever. I didn't care. I was so happy. I swear to god I'm bipolar.

And I assured him that he wouldn't have to worry

about a thing. That I'd buy everything, that he'd just have to wear it. It was going to be perfect. Like it was meant to be. And before I even knew what the hell was coming out of my mouth, I lied, and I tell him that my middle name's Kristen. That we'd be like Kristen and Robert, like Bella and Edward. It's like I can't believe all the synchronicity.

And it's not like I look like her, and I don't even think she's that pretty anyways, but I've been told that I have the exact same profile as Kristen Stewart. And it's true. If you like took a picture of my head and stuck it on the poster, you couldn't tell the difference. I've checked in the mirror even.

So we wound up at this Halloween party. Like a house party, a costume party, after the bar. Tyler knows some girl who was invited, and she tells us all to come. I don't know her. She's dressed up like a slutty devil and is real drunk. It's ok if we don't have a costume, she says.

And for like how popular the movies and books are, I'm surprised at how many people ask us what we're dressed up as. It's weird. Like we're hidden in plain sight. No one knows who we are, and no one knows who we're supposed to be.

And it's like I didn't know what the hell was going on. I mean, I kept turning my head to people, like talking sideways to them, showing my profile. I added more glitter to Robert. Nothing. Nothing worked. So I tell Robert to keep his mouth open, so like his fangs will show, and he isn't even wearing them. What the hell?

It's too hard, he says, he drools too much or some shit. He can't drink with the fangs in his mouth. I just scowled at him. I scowled at him and his lame excuses. His stinking thinking. And I took off to find a drink. I was so fucking mad I didn't even care if he caught me drinking straight out of a bottle.

By the time I finished my drink and got back, Robert was gone. I was like looking all over the place and I couldn't see him, but then I found Tyler across the room. So I ask him if he's seen Robert. And he says he's not sure, but he thinks he popped out for a smoke. Says he looked kind of choked, like he wanted to leave. Maybe he already took off? Said some shit about how he didn't want to wear his fangs anymore.

And then Tyler tells me that this girl, Alethea, who works at the Icarus, is shitfaced. I know who she is, but she probably doesn't know me. We're not friends. I worked with her idiot boyfriend for a little while a couple of years ago. And I saw her there, all drunk and gross, dressed up like a hooker pirate. Tyler says that she's like all falling over and laughing and saying stupid shit. Like she's flirting with everyone, acting real slutty, and she's probably going to get date raped or gang banged, she's so drunk.

Anyways, she was laughing and trying to figure out who Robert was dressed up as. She can barely stand and she's squinting and staring and trying to figure it out. And then she tells him that he looks familiar, like that actor, that actor with the teeth. Like she can't remember his name. He was in that movie—that one with the wood chipper. He's funny. He looks funny. And Tyler tells me that after a couple minutes, they figured it out.

And my mouth just dropped open. There is no way, there is no fucking way that Robert looks like Steve Buscemi. Alethea wishes she could fuck Robert—he's gorgeous. She's just jealous because her boyfriend Dennis is gross. He thinks he's like a bodybuilder, but really he's just fat and he's going bald and has tits and backne. He's always wearing tight golf shirts with sweat rings under his arms, and baggy pyjama pants that are way too tight on his ass. Like they run up his crack. Just too nasty. I once saw him pose for a picture at work. He was like doing a side shot, pointing at the ground with both hands, going, Is there gum on my shoe? Is there gum on my shoe? He was like flexing his tits and triceps and lifting his heel. Like doing some gross muscleman pose. It was unreal. And he drives around in his Hummer, up and down the same street like a half dozen times, with his R&B cranked so you can hear it a block away. Trying to impress the teenage girls or some shit.

No wonder Alethea was being such a slut. No wonder she wanted to get gang raped. I was going to have some words with her. Teach her a fucking lesson. But Tyler was blocking me, saying he shouldn't have told me, like almost begging me to calm down.

Then poor Boo showed up and wanted to know what was going on. So Tyler tells him, and Robert tries to talk me down, tells me to think of the baby. He's all like, You don't want to get kicked in the belly when you're having a baby, do you? You'll hurt the baby... the baby can drop out. Just don't worry about it... just calm down... Come on, think of the baby...

He was right. And then he put his fangs back in, like to cheer me up, to calm me down—and I cooled off right away. I knew how much he hated those fangs. It was like one of the nicest things anybody's done for me in a long time. So I tell him not to worry about it—Edward doesn't even have fangs anyways—don't worry about it, it's ok. And I give him a big hug.

And when I let go of him, he takes the fangs out of his mouth, and he gives me this look—I don't even know what kind of look he's giving me. He just takes a long pull on his beer and he doesn't take his eyes off me. He was probably just real drunk. I don't know, I was just so happy to have such an awesome boyfriend. Like for real—who gives a shit if some drunk skank thinks he looks gross?

And whatever, it was like no big deal—I could always get Alethea later. I know where she works. I could find out what she drives.

# THREE

# el Rapo

He says that Poon is a for real last name, that a lot of people have it. I tell him that I like Stanley J. Poon, I love Arnold J. Poon, and that Ronald J. Poon is growing on me. But really I don't understand any of this and I'm just trying to be helpful.

Robert's pretty happy with his story, says that Tyler helped him a lot. Like gave him some ideas and pointers and shit. Said it needed a prologue, something to get the action set up. He even wrote most of it. Robert really appreciated the help because Tyler's kind of busy writing a tv script. It's called *Nick of Time*. He says that Tyler always had the title, but came up with the ideas later.

At first *Nick of Time* was about this cop, Officer Nikodemedus, who can like see the future. I guess he's got this bullet or rebar stuck in his head or some shit, and the chunk of metal gives him hallucinations. Only they're not hallucinations—he gets like visions of brutal murders that haven't happened yet. Like future murders. And he's got to like figure out the crimes before they happen so he can save the victims before they get killed.

But Tyler scrapped that idea. He figures people want to watch shows about supernatural islands. So *Nick of Time* is about this guy, Nick, who has like this time machine. Nick's really rich because he's always winning the lottery. He uses his lotto winnings to buy an island and make a reality tv show. It's called *Murder Island*. He travels back in time to catch people like Adolf Hitler and Jack the Ripper and Gandhi, and then he throws them all on this island with modern day death row inmates—like gangsters and serial killers. They run around raping and killing each other and create a society. None of them can escape the island or their heads will like blow up, and they have to be extra careful not to get eaten by the velociraptors.

Robert loves the idea, and says he wishes *Murder Island* was a real tv show. But I don't know. I'm not so sure. It bothers me. It reminds me of something Dean said a couple months back. I'm sure he was serious. It was late at night, and *Groundhog's Day* was on tv. I love Bill Murray. And Dean—I swear to god he wasn't even trying to be funny—he was just smiling and takes a sip of his beer, and he makes this gross sucking squeak sound through his snaggleteeth, and he's all like, If I could do that—redo the same day every day, or if I could travel around, like travel back and forth in time—I'd rape everything. Even the animals. Bill Murray could get away with raping everything... I don't know why he doesn't.

For real, I don't know why I hang out with these idiots.

DANGER IN THE LAND OF THE TURBAN
A SHEP AND CHET NOVEL

*By Stanley J. Poon*

PROLOGUE

San Francisco Harbor, Pier 51,
March 15, 1977, 3:00 am

Harry Twaddle ran. Not like he was jogging or like he was training for the San Francisco Marathon. Not even close. Harry Twaddle wasn't the athletic type. Truth be told, Harry Twaddle was a fat son of a bitch who only got off his miserable ass to get to the fridge, barstool, or whorehouse. Hell, he was so lazy he even owned a couple of bedpans—one for the bed and one for the couch. No, Harry wasn't running for fun or for exercise—Harry Twaddle was running for his goddamn life.

He was tangled up in so many Gordian Knots of bullshit and trouble that not even all the seventy-three thousand little pricks at the '73 Boy Scouts Jamboree at Farragut and Moraine State Parks could ever untie them. What a mess, he thought. Why did he ever get involved in this? Why? He should have known better. Only he knew damn well why—he was a sucker for a beautiful woman. Poor Linda, poor smoking hot Linda. She'd only asked him to investigate the disappearance of her father... get a bit of media attention... stir things up a little... and now she was... dead... a suicide they called it.

To Hell with it, he thought, all this running was bullshit. Harry was exhausted, he out of breath. He needed a smoke. So he stopped, wheezing, and lit a cigarette. He'd walk for a minute or two... just for a minute... he had a terrible stitch in his side... he'd walk off the cramps... just for a minute... and then he'd run again...

Harry rounded a corner, into an alley.

The cigarette dropped from his stunned open

mouth.

He stood face to face with his pursuer—inches from him—he damn well nearly bumped into him.

"No... no... it can't be... You—you're not real... you're..."

Harry stopped talking. A paralytic venom was injected into his neck—a poison that also had the peculiar side effect of amplifying nerve sensitivity by ten times. And in his last moments, Harry wished he had applied himself more in his high school physical education classes. *With all due respect Mr. Ladorski,* he'd asked, *When will I ever need PE in real life?* If only he could go back in time and tell himself *March 15, 1977, that's when, you little know-it-all son of a bitch bastard.*

It was an excruciating end, a real lousy way to go.

His damned ten-times-hyper-sensitive ears would be ringing and bleeding if he were able to scream.

CHAPTER ONE

Gavin McLeod, Coroner of the San Francisco Bay area, stood over the body. A good portion of his chili dog splattered on the ground. It was hard to tell one chunky mess from the other. One was made of beans, pig lips and assholes—the other had been the victim's rectal cavity in better times.

"Bruce, you wanna grab me the tongs? I think I found his wallet."

"Jesus Christ, McLeod," said the rookie, trying his damnedest not to gag, "how the Hell can you eat? The smell..."

McLeod ignored him, and carefully prodded the defiled anus as he took the last bites of his dog. He handled the tongs like a man who had been playing Operation all his life, not like the drunk who'd finished a forty of single malt scotch just hours before.

McLeod retrieved the wallet. Sticky strings of maybe blood trailed from it like hot mozzarella off a slice of Papa Antonio's pepperoni pizza.

"Looks like we got a Mr. Harold J. Twaddle... forty three years of age... eighteen dollars... press card... the man was a journalist."

Two men seemed to approach from nowhere.

"Outta the way, rookie."

Shep shoved Bruce out of the way, his partner Chet laughed.

"What have we got here, McLeod? This guy's a fucking mess."

McLeod wadded up a note that had been in Twaddle's hand and tossed it to Shep.

Shep easily snatched it out of the air and read it aloud.

"Goodbye, cruel world. I am sorry."

The detectives smirked.

"Hell of a way to kill yourself..." said Chet. "or a killer with a sense of humor..."

"Maybe," said McLeod, "but one thing's for sure... this poor bastard *was raped to death*."

The men eyed the messy asshole.

"Well son of a bitch..." said Bruce to himself. "I guess the old bastard really did see something."

"You got a witness?" said Shep.

"Yeah, some old bum, sent him to the drunk tank. Says he saw something—like a dog, only it was green, and it stank... gave off this horrible musk. Says it jumped on Twaddle. Twaddle fell and didn't get up. Then he says this thing stood on its hind legs. And at first he thought it was the tail—only it wasn't, because it was on the front—it uncoiled like one of those party blowers... and then the thing was on top of him again. And the eyes... he says the eyes reflected like an animal's in the dark. Reflected red. When the thing looked back at him, he says he thought he was going to die. The old bastard turned around and staggered away as fast as he could."

"...El Chupacabra..." said Chet as he stroked his moustache.

"Bullshit. This wasn't done by any animal... since when do animals leave suicide notes and calling cards?"

McLeod threw his half smoked cigarette on the ground, and bent over the body. He lifted up Harold Twaddle's shirt. A name had been violently scratched into his back.


el RAPO

# Ripley

Where the hell did I put it? I looked all over the place for it—like I must have pulled my jacket inside out like a dozen times. Seriously, how many fucking pockets or purses could have I lost it in? I dropped it at the party it is what happened. I mean, I was drunk. I've lost all sorts of shit when I'm drunk. It's not like I put it through the wash or threw it in the garbage or some shit. But whatever—it didn't matter how I lost it—I couldn't find her card anywhere.

I got it at the Halloween party. A little after I cornered and smacked Alethea and told her to fuck off before I killed her. Some drunk girl came up to me. I didn't know her but she thought she knew me. She was calling me Miranda, asking me if I still see Hannah around. How was Devin? Was I still working at the Poppy Seed? Still living at the Reprise? And I'm all like, Ya... Ya, same old. And she asks me some more shit, but I really can't hear her—it's loud and she's drunk. Mostly I just nod and smile and answer ya and laugh with her.

And then she's all like, Hey, have you met my cousin? And she points to some girl across the room talking to a few people. The girl's not overly animated. She's more cool, friendly, relaxed. Confident. Everyone's paying attention to her, like she's telling the most interesting story in the world. And then she smiles and says something and makes a couple of charming gestures, and everyone's laughing.

The drunk girl tells me to hang on a second—she'd be right back. I didn't hear what her emergency was, but I take her word for it, it's real important.

I watched her cousin. She had dark long hair, she was beautiful. Probably thirty, but looked mid-twenties. I already knew her without even talking to her. We had a lot of the same interests. Bought the same yoga pants. The same coffees and teas. Loved the same books and movies. But that's where it ended. She had all the advantages. Traveled all over the world. Surfing, skiing, drinking. Flamenco dancing in Spain. Living carefree, following her muse. She had a loving family that encouraged and supported her, financially and emotionally, even if she'd fuck up—but she never did. She'd also had fun at college or university, maybe even got a degree. Had a large support system, made lots of friends. You'd resent her—for all her beauty and success, for how life came so easy to her, how she drifted so effortlessly—if she wasn't such a likable person, if you didn't want to try so hard to impress her. I hated her already and we hadn't even met.

The drunk girl got back quick and babbled something about how she was sorry and then she grabbed my arm and dragged me, and was all like, Come on, you've got to meet her, come on. So she was pulling me and staggering and slurring some more shit. And then we get to her cousin and she introduces me, but I instantly forget her name and can't really hear much, it's so loud. This is Miranda, she's like my best friend... blahblahblah... school... blahblahblah... The Poppy Seed. I'm sure she's making us out to be better friends than we really are. Then the drunk girl's cousin smiles, and extends her hand, says nice to meet you or some shit. I give her hand a shake, and I notice that her face is covered in blood.

And I'm all like, Wow, your costume is so gross.

I sounded like a retard. I couldn't think of anything else to say. But it was a real good costume. I hadn't even noticed it until she was right in front of me. She was like wearing cargo pants and suspenders and a tight white T-shirt, which was splattered in blood and had that alien from the movies popping out of her belly. And I didn't come right out and ask her, because maybe it was part of her costume or maybe she just had a fat gut, but she looked pregnant. And after spending the next fifteen, twenty minutes listening to these people, I found out that she was. The skinny bitch was about six, seven months in, but she looked more like four. Why the hell did I get so fucking fat?

My best friend disappeared again. So I started talking to her cousin. I tell her that I'm pregnant too, just over six months, same as her. And she's all like, Oh wow, I would never have noticed. So I start talking diet with her, and then we talk more pregnant shit. She's doing most of the talking, but she's asking me a lot of questions too, like she's genuinely interested. Mostly I just nod and agree with her and laugh and say ya ya, and, oh I know, *I know*, and, for sure, for sure.

Ripley's trying to figure out what I'm dressed up as, and I'm all like, Oh, nothing... it was a stupid idea, nobody knows who we are. And I explain to her that I'm here with my boyfriend, and that he's supposed to be Edward and I'm pregnant Bella. It's stupid, I say, it was a stupid idea. And then she's all like, Oh my god, of course, of course! That's so good! And it's not like she was just saying that to be nice. She even knows the scene the cos-

tumes are from. And then she's all like, I hope you don't
mind my saying this—and I don't know if anybody's ever
told you this before—but from the side... you look just
like Kristen Stewart.

That settled it. I needed to have this girl as my friend.
Maybe I had her all wrong, like I was too quick to judge—
I mean she was so pretty. And even though I probably
still hated her just a little in the back of my mind, I
wanted her to like me. I needed her approval.

And then some Thai hooker interrupted us and says
some shit into Ripley's ear. There must have been like
fifty girls dressed as hookers at the party. Bunch of sluts.

So Ripley says she's sorry, she's got to go. Some girl
named Zoey—who I'm guessing is her drunk cousin—my
best friend—is puking and passed out in the shitter.
She's got to get her cleaned up and drive her home. She
says it was really nice meeting me, and she hands me a
card. Then she apologizes—she's not trying to be tacky
and get business, but it has her number on it. She says to
call her anytime and leave a message if I want—we'll go
for tea.

And then she fucked off, like Cinderella or some shit.
And I lost the glass slipper.


## iPhone


This girl from work, Kameljit Guptha, tried to kill herself
today.

The janitor, I don't know his name, slithered up to us
in the coffee room. So gross. He creeps me out. When he

looks at me I feel like he wants to rape me. Like he wants to kill me. Keep me in his fridge. Eat my skin.

Does anybody speak... *Hindu?* he says.

Ya. Ya I fucking speak *Hindu*. What a fucking retard. He looks it too, with his rat face and crossed eyes. I don't even know which one to look at. He wears a Playboy Bunny necklace, fingerless gloves, and a belt with so much shit attached to it I don't know how his pants stay up. You should see his backpack. There's like a 7-11 coffee mug the size of a midget attached to it. He's going to get scoliosis or whatever, I swear. But hey, at least he's ready for any situation, with all his pliers and duct tape and shit. Except for translation, I guess.

He found Kameljit on the floor of the women's shitter. And I felt a little bad. She'd been by my desk earlier asking if I had any painkillers. I had some Midol in my drawer. I shot her the bottle. And I also gave her an Adderall, a Percocet, an Ativan, a Zoloft and one of my leftover rave pills if she needed anything else. I mean, I didn't know—I was just trying to help. And Nancy—whose hair's just a total disaster—tells us that she took like sixteen pills. And I don't know how she knew this, but I didn't doubt it. Nancy's like a total nosy cunt—the kind of bitch who knows everyone and reads the obituaries every week to see who died. For real, her hair looked crazy and whorish. I had to look away.

Poor Kameljit. I wondered if she'd ever listened to the cds I'd burned for her. Probably not. A couple of the girls wondered if she was just doing all this for attention. Probably not. I mean, I know—I've done it for attention, and I don't think she was faking it.

Nancy says that Kameljit threw all her savings into

Sun Money Systems International. Like sixty, seventy thousand maybe. Like all her life's savings. Money that she was supposed to like buy a husband with. Like a dowry? Only now she had nothing, or she couldn't get at her money, and her parents had some stud lined up for her in India. Nancy says that if her parents found out, they'd like beat the brown off her, or throw acid in her face or some shit. They'd be like so ashamed and dishonored.

And I guess that when the paramedics wheeled her out, Nancy was like standing behind a plant or some shit, watching, listening. She said that Kameljit was like crying, like all quiet, and just kept on going, Please... I'm ok... I'm ok now... just don't tell my father... please... please don't tell my father...

I really wish she'd listened to those cds. I couldn't imagine like *for real* trying to kill myself. Some people have real problems.

This asshole I used to work with at another job called me Karoshi. Thought it was funny. Like he'd call me it to my face. I didn't know what it meant at first, but it's like Japanese for *death by overwork*. For serious. They actually work themselves to death so much over there that they made a word for it. The Japanese have got all sorts of words for retarded ways to kill yourself.

And you want to know why I just bought an iPhone? Because karoshi. The guys who make the iPhones for Steve Jobs in like China or whatever take it very seriously. They are committed to making the best phones possible. It's like the worst thing in the world for them be lazy and make a shitty phone. They do not want to appear foolish in front of Mr. Steve Jobs. To look like a fat lazy retard in front of Mr. Steve Jobs. To take advantage of the good graces and generosity of Mr. Steve Jobs. It would like bring dishonor and shame to themselves, to their good family name, and to the ghosts of their ancestors. Or some shit like that.

Anyways, there was a bunch of losers that like flung themselves out of the third floor windows or roofs of the iPhone factory. Like so many of them that they actually for real put nets around all the buildings. Like the pressure to keep up and perform was too much for some to handle. One kid left a note saying he had no capabilities, that he made shitty phones, that he got what he deserved. Another jumped because he got his bonus stolen. I would never kill myself over work. I'd rather quit. I couldn't think of anything more retarded to kill yourself over. But you have to admire the work ethic that goes into these phones.

This is why I also don't mind buying sweat shop products. Fear and desperation and a dream of a better life produce quality results. Like fear of getting fired. Fear of getting burned or beaten. Fear of being sacrificed, your head put in a kiln. Fear of paying your loan shark, so he doesn't sell your ten year old's ass to sleazy tourists. I'm not even making this shit up. Some fat lazy union worker doesn't give a shit if my tv works or not. He's just wondering where he's going to go for beer and hot wings after work. It's true.

And it's like I just don't get it. How many people put that much effort into getting what they want out of life? Like would like risk everything for what was *best for them?* I mean, I don't know. And I honestly don't care. But whatever. Cycle of life or some shit.

Anyways, the attempted suicide was all anybody would talk about. It was like everyone was so serious, so miserable. Like you couldn't escape it. So I thought it might be kind of funny if I emailed memos to the staff. Like a joke. Cheer up the glum idiots. So I wrote this one on like company protocol and best practices for suicide. It was pretty good, I've typed up all sorts of memos.

Dear Staff,

In light of recent events, we at Petrus Cheong and Associates Global want to remind you that due to third party insurance policy issues, suicide *for personal reasons* is to be carried out *off company property and outside of company time.*
If the attempted suicide is *work related,* for reasons such as—but not limited to—lack of productivity, or truancy, it is recommended that it *be carried out at designated and marked jump windows and not on premises.*
Your assistance in this matter is greatly appreciated.

Thank You.
—Management.

I guess somebody didn't think it wasn't very funny and ratted me out. What a waste of a half hour. So Kim—who is a guy—and Felix and Brooke sit me down in, I don't know, like one of their offices. And they have actual for real papers on company policy and codes of conduct that they want me to read and sign and shit. And I just start bawling, like I'm not even listening it them, and I'm all like, I'm sorry, it's just me and Kameljit are such close friends... we went for lunch together... this is just so weird.

I must have looked like a mess I was crying so much. And then I was going on about how it's just hard because I'm pregnant, how I'm on medication, how I was molested as a child, how I tried to kill myself, how I have body issues.

I was throwing anything at them and they were doing their best to calm me down. Like, It's ok, it's ok, it's not your fault. We're not blaming you... we just need you to be clear on... to understand... company policy. So we're all on the same page going forward. Just read the pamphlet. Sign the policy form... it's no one's fault... this is all just sad and tragic... no one's in any trouble... we just all need everyone to be... *clear.*

They knew they fucked up and just want to get me out of the office as quick as possible. Management don't want to deal with a psychotic emotional wreck. They hide all day to avoid conflict.

So I kind of get a grip and I apologize again. I tell them how much I enjoy working at Petrus Cheong and Associates Global. How much I appreciate the job that all of them and all of the other managers are doing. And how much I like Kameljit and that I'm sorry—I must be in shock. It won't happen again. I sign their form and grab the company propaganda. And I'm hoping they'll send me home, but they tell me it's ok if I want to go back to work. I wasn't going to push my luck.

But whatever, I didn't care. I just drew moustaches and buckteeth and glasses on the sensitivity training pamphlet crybabies. And then I went on Assbook for the last half of my shift. Monica was talking about her Down syndrome kid again, about some race he was going in. Sticking her hat out for donations. Andre was upset some girl didn't like him. Didn't like him or all the weird shit that he was sending her. Couldn't believe she wanted to slap a restraining order on him. And Nancy was busy giving live updates about her day at work. I swear to god that woman's hair is a nightmare. I wish I couldn't see her head from my desk.

## Wrong Place, Wrong Time

I got home from work and I was really upset. Robert doesn't say much. Like he doesn't say much to me, but he's a great listener, you know? He'll listen to me talk and talk and talk, and he won't say a word. It's like he'll never start a conversation with me. Like he's a for real strong silent type. You know that when he talks, it's like important.

He's also a real sensitive guy. Like an empath almost? His rivers run deep. He could tell that something was wrong with me. So he stops watching his, I don't know, hockey game? and asks if I'm ok. And I'm wiping the tears away from my eyes and I'm all like, Ya, ya I'm fine... No big deal. Just work.

But he can tell that I'm not ok. And it was just like so sweet. He pats the couch, like for me to come sit by him, and when I do, he puts his arm around me and rubs my shoulders. And then he's all like, Do you want to talk about it? What's the matter? And I'm all like, No, it's nothing. Don't worry about it—your game is on. I'm fine.

I'm ok.

And he's all like, No, it's ok, it's intermission anyways. Tell me... tell me what's wrong.

So I like tell him about my shitty day at work. How my bosses were mean to me and I'll be so glad when I don't have to go back to that... that hellhole. How everybody hates it there and hates each other and how it sucks and I can't wait until I'm done.

And he tells me that I'm lucky to have a good job. That *he's* lucky I have a good job. And then he goes on about this game that he plays whenever he has a bad day at work. It's called *Wrong Place, Wrong Time.* Before that he used to just stare at the mirror and cut his face with a razor.

He says that when he gets angry, he'll just bottle it up. And then maybe on his coffee break or lunch, or whenever he gets a chance, he'll drive somewhere. Or for the last year or so, walk somewhere. And then he'll just stop. Usually when he calms down a bit. Like when his vision isn't so blurry, or when he stops shaking, or stops yelling and swearing at himself. It could be anywhere. A bus stop. A park bench. A DQ parking lot. A high school. And he'll pull the blade out on his knife and hold it in his jacket pocket.

And the next person he sees—it's always got to be an attractive young woman—he'll like imagine abducting her at knifepoint. He'll like throw her in the back of his van. Torture her. Rape her. Beat her. And she'll cry and beg him to let her go, like she'll promise she won't tell the police. Only he has to kill her, because she's seen his face. Usually by strangulation, but sometimes if she struggles, like puts up a fight, he'll stab her with the same knife that she stuck in his side or his leg.

And then he gets all *CSI* and thinks of ways to safely get rid of the body, like where to dump it, how to speed up decomposition, shit like that. And usually when he gets to that part he forgets what got him so angry or stressed and he already feels better.

And I tell him that his game is fucking disgusting, and that I don't like him thinking of other girls that way. That I'm like really sickened, like real disappointed. That he'd better stop it and buy some more weed. It's gross. And he totally backpedals and says this is something he did like three, four years ago. That he learned better anger management tools in his court appointed courses. Like *Hand of God*. Where before you get road rage, you like swat or crush or flick cars with your giant hand, using perspective and your imagination.

I tell him that one sounds better. I might try that one, it sounds like fun. For real—I can't believe how many shitty drivers there are out there.


## GOOP


I love Gwyneth Paltrow. I fucking *love* her. I love GOOP. And I wanted to do something nice for Boo. Like make him dinner. It's seems he's always eating fast food garbage when I get home from work. Anyways, Robert was doing a bit of drywall packing, like under the table, and I wanted to make sure it was ready for him when he got home.

I was reading this recipe for pizza that looks really

nice. Gwyneth recommends using a wood burning stove if you've got one. She says that one of the best things she's ever done is build a wood burning stove in her backyard. Gwyneth's got this great let them eat cake attitude, which I love. I imagine one day me and Robert will have a wood burning stove and a back yard, but until then, she says it's ok to use a pizza stone in your oven. Any way you slice it, she says, homemade pizza cannot be beat.

But I don't know. The pizza looks tricky. Like lots of prep and stuff. I haven't kneaded dough since high school. And I don't know if Robert would really appreciate a Margherita pizza anyways. But the pictures of the pizza making—like the directions and stuff—are gorgeous. There's even a shot of one burnt pizza, which I don't think I could take after putting in all that effort. It would all be too much, my heart would break. No sweat for Gwyneth, though. She cracks a charming joke about having too much beer and it's all good.

I wish I could meet her, hang out with her, be like best friends. I'm pretty sure we'd get along great—we have so much in common. It's like she's my sister or something. Like what she eats, what she wears, her interests—she does the same things that I want to do. It's weird. Sometimes she'll like share a blog entry on something that I was just thinking about or dreaming about the day before, and I'll be all like, Yes... Yes!...Exactly... *Exactly!* Like she's reading my mind. Or like we share the same mind. Or we're the same person.

And looking at all these photos I imagine me, Gwyneth, Mario Batali and Jamie Oliver. Like all sitting in her beautiful back yard, eating her Quattro Formaggi pizza—

which I'm sure would be my favorite it looks so good. We'd be like talking about parenting, and Tuscany, and food, and laughing and having the best time.

And then I'm not so sure. Like I'm changing my mind. Like I'm starting to think that I don't want Jamie Oliver there anymore. He's a little bit of a fucking crybaby—for real. I mean, I'm into healthy eating and all that shit too, but just the way he goes on and on with his food revolution. Like he's always sobbing... the children... obesity... heart disease... type II diabetes...

I once heard a rumor that he was at this Chinese nail salon when he was in town doing a book signing or promoting a show or some shit. And he just starts weeping and shrieking because some girl filed his nails down a little shorter than he liked. And this poor girl doesn't speak English. Fresh off the boat. She's just terrified. Like they'll send her back to China, or put her in jail, or she'll have to become a hooker or some shit. She doesn't know. And he like refuses to pay them. He's sobbing. Like his lips are pulled back so you can see all his English teeth and gums. He says he wants them *do it right*. Like give him clip-ons to make them a sixteenth of an inch longer or some crazy shit. How am I supposed to cook with these nails? he keep whining.

My friend says that she was there. That it's true. Or I don't know—maybe it was a rumor I made up at the bar? Or at work? Whatever, I can't remember anymore. But I wouldn't doubt that it was true. I wouldn't doubt it at all.

So I looked for something easier to prepare. I tried out Gwyneth's Best Dirty Martini—which is excellent, exactly how I like mine—and I read more GOOP. I read about Gwyneth's gross sweaty seat filler who left her seat all wet and sweaty at the Emmys. I read The Cheese Board. I read about Homosexuality in the Bible.

And then I just said fuck it and ordered a pizza. It was kind of getting too late to throw something together for poor Boo. He'd probably like the Pizza Hut better anyways. I made a note to myself to buy Gwyneth's cookbook *My Father's Daughter*. I was going to start cooking more. I really was going to be the best mother. And one of these days, the best wife. I really was. I knew it.

I also decided that I needed to write to or contact Gwyneth. Like maybe start some sort of correspondence. A blog? I wasn't sure, but I make friends pretty easy.

## Loft

You should see it, he tells me. It's so cool. It's amazing. It's like you're really flying a plane. Robert can't stop smiling. I wonder how the hell he knows what it's like to really fly a plane. I wonder why he thinks I want to hear about it for like the tenth time.

He tells me that Tyler's brother, Josh, made a lot of money selling his half of some internet company or whatever. Like four hundred thousand dollars. He works in some computer department at the university now. More money. So he gets this downtown loft and starts ordering all sorts of crazy shit. Like a flight simulator. Like an actual flight simulator with a moving cockpit and a flight simulator program. With all the real switches and panels and everything. It's so real that the government did a background check on him to make sure he wasn't going to like fly it into a building or up the President's asshole or some shit.

And I feel like Robert's more excited about the stupid video game than he is about having a baby. Like he's more interested in hanging out with his friends than he is with me. So I tell him. I tell him that it would be nice if he showed that much enthusiasm about having a baby. Even just once.

And then he gets all defensive and is all like, Well I, uh... you know... you never tell me anything about your pregnant stuff. Like ultrasounds or doctor shit. Like am I supposed to go to the doctor with you? I don't know... do you need me to, I don't know, do anything? Like classes or anything? Because I mean, I will... it's just that... I don't know. I'm sorry... I just don't know what I'm supposed to be doing. I thought you'd be telling me more...

I tell him it's ok. I'm just hormonal, I guess. Don't worry about it. I just thought we might be seeing more of each other after we'd moved in together is all. He can go fly his plane.

I honestly think I used to see more of him when we were both working full time and living apart. I've barely seen him the last couple weeks. Ever since he returned the favor and helped Tyler and Josh move, he's barely been home. It's like all he does now is hang out at the loft with his friends and play video games and smoke weed. Or jam in the soundproof music room. Or use the home gym and MMA training area. Or watch movies in the home theatre.

I couldn't compete. Seriously. Especially since he wouldn't touch me. And it's not like I was going to keep blowing him for no good reason. I don't know, it's almost like I missed Dean and his dirty couch. Like maybe it was Dean's bad influence, like his radioactive pheromones. Like they just poisoned Robert, dragged him down to his lazy level. Like his Kundalini asshole chakra just sucked and drained all the life and energy out of the room and kept Robert at home. I don't know.

Whatever. I was going to the Snail and Rooster. Stripper night. They could crash that fucking flight simulator for all I cared. There just better not be any little bitches hanging out at that loft. If I ever find out there's any little bitches there, I'll burn that fucking place to the ground.


## Dear Red Shoes


There are a lot of stupid girls out there. Like *a lot* of stupid girls. And I wanted to do something good. Like to help them. I kind of believe that the more good we do for others, the more good comes back to us. Like karma, I guess. So I put these ads up on Craigslist and shit, with a link to an Assbook account that I made especially for the ads. I called myself Red Shoes.

I kind of got the idea, like the inspiration, from *Red Shoe Diaries*. You know, softcore porn, light jazz, sax. David Duchovny and his dog Stella go to the post office and read these pervy letters that women send him in response to a personal ad requesting pervy letters from women. It was a pretty good show.

Anyways, I figured there are a lot of girls who, you know, go to prom and they're pregnant and maybe they don't even know they're pregnant. And they have the baby in the school's shitter, except for they don't want the baby. Maybe they're confused. Maybe they thought they just had cramps, or ate some bad sushi or whatever. And now there's a baby in the toilet, and they don't know what to do. They just want to keep dancing and hanging out with their friends and having fun—only now they've got this baby in the shitter to deal with.

So they wrap the baby up in its cord and the towel from one of those gross cloth dispensers. The ones that are always like covered in green and yellow hork and blood and snot. And they'll toss the baby in the garbage can with the used tampons and shit. Then they'll go back out to the gym and shake their leaky ass with some other skanks, or maybe like the class clown, and their dance will wind up on YouTube or whatever.

It was these girls that I was hoping to reach. Or girls who knew that they were pregnant and really didn't want anything to do with it. Like maybe they couldn't afford to abort, or didn't want to because they're like religious, or feel sorry for the fetus or some shit.

So I put up a few ads.

LADIES—

> HAVE YOU HAD YOUR HEART BROKEN?
> DO YOU FEEL BETRAYED AND ALONE?
> ARE YOU PREGNANT AND
> DON'T KNOW WHERE TO TURN?
> I CAN HELP.

—RED SHOES

GIRLS—

ARE YOU PREGNANT? ALONE?
NOBODY KNOWS?
ARE YOU CONFUSED?
LOOKING TO ABORT?
STOP.
THERE ARE OTHER OPTIONS.
$$$$$$


—RED SHOES


The thing is, you try to do something good, something nice, and people take advantage. They think it's fucking funny. Like some big joke. It didn't take long for all the trolls to come out. And the religious people, who like wanted me to join their cults, or to protest in front of some gyno's or abortionist's office or some shit.

Everybody responded except for the girls that I was trying to help. I had to take down the ads, there was too much bullshit. Too many assholes. And I think the police were looking into it. Maybe I'd try again in a couple of weeks, without the Red Shoes.

I also tried to make some pregnant friends online. I switched from pregnationdivas.com to futuremilf.com. The website's way better, almost as nice as Prana's. There's like lots of discussions, lots of users and threads. The pictures are awesome too. Shit like a pregnant gut being held from behind by a pair of strong man hands. Black hands on a white belly. Very striking. Maybe like he's trying to steal the baby?—no he doesn't want it. There's one of like a lady pulling up her blouse to show off her pregnant gut, and she's like draping roses over it. There's hot pregnant women doing yoga on the beach. There's one of a pretty pregnant woman smiling and eating salad. And there's a nerdy hot girl with bangs, wearing dark rimmed glasses. She's curled up on a comfy chair, with her fat belly and a good book.

I found a few girls in my area, at nearly the same stage of pregnancy. I inboxed all of them a couple of times. You know, see if they wanted to get together, do whatever. Shoot the pregnant shit. Two girls responded. So I sent them each like another half dozen or so messages, seeing when they wanted to meet or get in touch. One girl put me on *Ignore* and the other girl canceled or changed her account. Whatever, I don't give a shit. They can get raped or stabbed in the gut for all I care. I got enough friends anyways.


# Phil Collins


I had no idea it was that bad. I mean, a couple of people in my building looked at me all weird on the way in. And my face felt puffy and my vision was getting blurry, but I had no idea it was that bad until Boo started freaking out. So then I looked in the mirror and I freaked out.

I'm not even lying. I looked like that dude with the big ginger head in *Mask*. That one with Cher in it. And she's got this retarded kid with a head the size of a watermelon. He like fucks this blind girl, like tricks her, because she can't see how ugly he is, and then he dies. It's pretty sad, and like a true story or some shit. But maybe I really

166

looked more like that gross thing in *The Goonies*. That thing that like kept cupping the fat kid's tits and licking his face on the pirate ship.

Anyways, it was that bad. Like for real. My face was swollen so much that my eyes were barely open. I was breaking out in hives and it was getting harder to breathe. I looked disgusting. I started to cry, I started to panic. I was hyperventilating. Boo calmed me down enough to convince me to follow him. When we got to the door I freaked out and told him I couldn't go outside looking like this. Like some hideous monster. He just grabbed his jacket and threw it over my head and told me he was driving me to the hospital. He told me that I had to calm down, that I had to calm down for our baby.

I didn't calm down, but he managed to drag me to the Escalade. And I don't know how many times he asked, but he was all like, What happened? What the hell happened? I was bawling and hysterical. And when I calmed down enough to hear him, I said it was a raccoon. Some raccoon in the alley that was digging around in a bucket of chicken. Washing a drum in a puddle with his quick little hands. And he went nuts, like freaked out when I got too close to his bucket. Started hissing, screeching. Beat the shit out of me.

I don't even know why I said it was a raccoon. I'd heard somewhere before that raccoons could be mean nasty creatures if provoked. But I've never seen one in the city.

So when we got into Emergency, Robert explained to the girl at the desk that I had been attacked by a raccoon. That it probably had some diseases, that something horrible was happening to me. I was pregnant, he told them. They needed to hurry. I felt bad for him. His story sounded insane. My poor Boo. The dirty looks and whispers he was getting in the ER.

I was lucky though. They got me in fast. The doctor was old. Like forty, fifty maybe. He had that longish curly hair that made him look like a dyke. He gave me some shots. Like some cortisone or antihistamines, and a tetanus shot. He checked my heart rate, blood pressure, the usual doctor shit. Cleaned the scratches on my face and tits. He told me he'd never dealt with raccoon attacks, but that the allergy symptoms should clear up soon, and that I'd probably have to get rabies shots as a precaution. I tell him not to worry about it, that I've had my rabies shots.

And I don't know why I lied, why I didn't tell Robert it was a cat. I mean, it was no big deal. I was out of my head, I guess. There's this cat, I don't know if he's like a stray or lives nearby, but he's a friendly cat, and he comes to the alley where I smoke at work. I don't smoke at our building anymore, because I don't need all the nasty stares and the judgement and gossip. And there's also this weird chick who comes by our building. She's like bald and real tall and fat. She wears a muumuu and walks around barefoot. Even in the cold and rain. She must be fucking nuts, or maybe she's a cancer patient. But she looks exactly like a grown baby, and she comes by our smoke pit every day and asks for a cigarette, and frowns like she's sad when you say no. Fuck her. She can go buy her own cigarettes, they're expensive.

Anyways, I smoke about a block away now, behind this cafe where this cat comes by, they're always leaving him food at the back door. I've seen other smokers pet him sometimes. They call him Mr. Hugginsauce. But I call him Phil, because he's got the Phil Collins airstrip on top of his head.

So I was having a smoke, and there was no one else around, just me and Phil, and I was scratching his airstrip. I picked him up and he was purring. And then, I don't know, I guess I was reaching, fumbling around in my handbag and I was trying to hold Phil with my left arm and it's just awkward. He's like adjusting his position. So when I pulled the knife out and tried to stab him, he kind of got all sketchy, like climbed up my shoulder, and I missed and cut his leg or tail and nearly stabbed myself.

So Phil freaks out. Just screeches and howls and claws at my face, and I drop the knife and try to rip him off. Only he's clawing my arms and tits and hair and I can't pry him loose. That cat really beat the shit out of me. And when he's nearly done killing me he jumps off and runs around the corner.

It was a stupid idea. Even if I had stabbed him, I would have gotten cat blood all over my jacket. I don't know what the hell I was thinking. And I kind of liked the cat, even.

Anyways, I was a mess. There was like no one in the alley, but I thought I heard the cafe door being unbolted. So I picked up my knife and my bag and I fucked off real quick. I called work and told them that I was sick, that I couldn't make it back in. My head was like dizzy. I knew I was allergic to cats, but I had no idea that it was that bad.

But honestly, at that moment, I was mostly worried that Phil had ruined my tattoo. If only it had been colder out and I'd buttoned up my jacket more. I have this beautiful black and white portrait of Oprah on my left tit, and that cat had absolutely mangled it.

## It's just water

I bought the baby some clothes. Real cute stuff. There was a pink shirt that said *In Your Wildest Dreams* that had like a fluffy sheep jumping a fence on it. There was a beautiful baby safe sequined one that said *Innie* on it, because there's no fucking way my baby's going to have some big ugly knob hanging off her belly like a penis. I'd cut that thing off with the razor myself.

I found them at the mall. Like when I was looking around for holiday ideas. Like for presents and shit. I kind of got it in my head that Robert would propose around Christmastime or New Year's, before the baby arrived. It only made sense. So I was looking at diamonds, like at rings. But I was just setting myself up for disappointment. Robert could never afford the ones that I wanted, like the ones big enough to see. And I felt this sudden overwhelming wave, like that I was going to start bawling, so I left.

There was a shitty looking guy outside the store, stooped over by the window, looking at his phone. He was taking pictures of this diamond poster—The Oracle Collection—and he was like all quiet, *How do you like me now? How do you like me now, bitch?*

Maybe it was just the holidays, but there was a lot of the mentally ill out. Like a guy who was six inches from a wall twisting his arms, doing a Balinese looking dance with his shadow. Some chick in a housecoat who looked normal but was whispering to a friend that wasn't there. And some Indian who I assumed was drunk at first, yelling at the top of his lungs, *Get off my bus! Get the fuck off my bus or I'll call the police!* There was no bus or anybody nearby except for me. I walked away faster and could still hear him yelling over a block away. But these lunatics made me feel better about myself. Like it didn't matter how lame my holidays were going to be, at least I wasn't them.

It's not like I was stressed though. A lot of people are stressed by the holidays, but not me. I was busy, for sure, but I really didn't give a shit if I got everything done or not. It's not like I was going to sweat my sack off over some dumb turkey or other bullshit. Fight with a bunch of retards in the mall over holiday gifts. Pregnancy was my excuse for everything now. I was like having a difficult one. And I didn't need the extra stress—or the baby might fall out or die in my womb.

And I didn't have any family for Christmas dinner anyways. I haven't spoken to my mom in years. The last time we talked, she didn't approve of my lifestyle. Like what I did for extra college money. There was a couple videos online, I guess. Some fucking perv she knows found them. And I was all like, It wasn't me, it wasn't me. I swore up and down it wasn't me. Only the girl looked exactly like me, and was wearing my high school cheerleader uniform. But whatever. I don't give a shit. If some geezer wants me to suck his gray old dick after it's been up my asshole and then drink his pee, fine—I'll take his three hundred and fifty bucks. It's just water.

So I was thinking of going to the staff Christmas party. It was a free dinner, free drinks. I could bring Boo if I wanted, but I'm pretty sure he wouldn't want to go. He'd be too busy. Hanging out at Tyler's, no doubt. Playing video games. Drinking and smoking. I don't know. Whatever. I wasn't even going to bother telling him. I'm getting too fat anyways. I don't want to like buy a dress that I'm never going to wear again. Maybe I'd just pop in for a few free drinks and leave.

Boo was leaving for Christmas. His parents bought him a ticket to go visit them for the holidays. I can't say I minded. Maybe they'd get me something nice. Have Robert bring it back for me. I mean, I don't know them—and have never like met or spoken to them—but you'd figure they would want to give the mother of their grandchild a nice Christmas gift. Unless they were like Jews or Jehovahs or some shit

And honestly, I was looking forward to having the place to myself. Robert was getting to be a real fucking slob. Seriously. Like leaving his smelly socks and beer cans and shit all over the place. Letting his dirty dishes pile up. I was getting real sick of nagging him and throwing all his shit in the garbage. His mother can clean up after his lazy ass for a week.

He was kind of excited though. Like he'd heard about all the shit that the New Year's baby was going to get. Free diapers for a year, free baby food, free money. Liquorshack was giving away a case of champagne. The zoo was offering to take a pictures of the baby with new white lion cubs. There was like three of them, they were so cute.

I broke it to him that it wasn't going to happen. End of

January, maybe February if I felt like it. And he just gave me this look—like devastated—like the retarded kid who just found out the hard way you can't play that rough with your new puppy. I felt horrible for him.

I still haven't figured out what to get him for Christmas yet. But I'm not too worried about it. I don't know, his jeans are getting pretty gross.

## The cyclists are gay

I hit this cyclist on the way to work today. It was no big deal, really. I mean, I think I more like clipped him. It was an accident. But he was an idiot anyway. Seriously, who the fuck rides a bicycle in the winter? I guess he didn't like that I drove too close to him or some shit and he like fingered and yelled at me. Like he feels brave yelling at a girl. So I turned right when he was going straight and he smashed into my car like a retard. I ran over the front of his bike and dragged it for half a block maybe. Some of his cyclist friends stopped to help him and were all like freaking out. I wasn't going to turn around to see if he was ok. It's not like I'm a fucking doctor.

Whatever, I didn't care. It was all good. I checked the Escalade and there were like no dents or scratches. I went online to check the local news, traffic reports, police scanners. Nothing. I was pretty sure I was in the clear. I felt better, a little relieved. And you know what? I was glad I hit him. It was the right thing to do, like Karma. Teach Asshole a lesson. Honestly, I hate the cyclists.

The cyclists are gay. I mean, I guess not all of them are, but it's like ninety percent ruin it for the rest of them.

They think that they are better than us. Like they're doing us all a big favor by riding their bikes. Like they're saving the planet. Like we owe them or some shit. They should go live in a country where people have real problems.

I don't like their Lycra. I don't like their helmets. I don't like their big legs and skinny arms. I don't like their swag. I don't like how they all take steroids and shit and lie about not taking them. I don't like how they stink when they get to work. I don't like how they ride on sidewalks and run reds and don't signal and go wherever they want. And I absolutely hate how they hog the lanes. Like it would kill them to move over a few inches. Like they're the ones paying the gas taxes and the carbon taxes. It's like they just don't give a shit. Like they're a real fuck-you-society.

I was walking by this greenspace a couple of months ago. I saw some dumb bitch training her child to ride a bike. Another fucking cyclist. I can't tell you how  much this kid sucked. The little girl was riding a bike with training wheels that had no business having training wheels anymore. And mom's all like, You can do it! I'm your biggest fan! I'm your biggest cheerleader! S-A-G-E... Sage! I wanted to puke. I wanted to shove that little animal off the bike. It's not like she did anything special. Most kids that age can ride bikes without training wheels. No wonder they all grow up feeling entitled, like it's ok to do whatever they want. Selfish pricks.

And this is the problem. There are a lot of lame parents. Like *a lot* of lame parents. They think it's all about them. Like they can take their screaming brat anywhere, that no one will mind. Like they can pull their ugly tit out and everybody had just better accept it. Like the world needs to change for them or some shit.

At least one of them got road rash on their balls today.

I looked at some exercise routines online. New Year's was coming up, and I for sure needed to lose some weight. I looked through *Urban Baby Mother*. I was pretty sure that I was going to enroll in a baby massage class. I read about breast feeding and peanut butter—like the dangers. And I read how some crazy British bitch wrote a book about skipping the puree stage of feeding. I also read about plagiocephaly, like how a baby could get a flat head. It was usually a lazy baby with low muscle tone. I was definitely going to sign us up for the mother/infant yoga class. I wasn't going to have a flat headed freak.

I decided that I was going to leave work sick for the rest of the day. I finished the jar of Little Monkey *Banana Kiwi Mush*. It was pretty good, but I like the Little Monkey *Banana Berry Lime* a little better. So far, the Baby Foodie *Peaches and Cream Dream* is my favorite. This other shit I tried, Baby Planet *Apple Pear Puree* tastes like shit. Like green chalky pear shit.


# Returnal


The young man at the counter looked very gay. He was leaning on it with one elbow, looking at his nails, and lisping into the phone. Probably talking about some gay shit. Maybe to his boyfriend. His skinny ass stuck out like he was looking to get it filled. He was arching his back like any good porn director would tell his actress to do.

So I was like looking around, acting all casual, waiting for him to get off the phone. And then he's all like, I'd better go, Gerald, ok, ok, I'll talk to you later, goodbye, yup, me too, ok, bye.

And then he smiles and asks if he can help me.

I don't know what the hell Robert was thinking. Like he felt guilty about us not fucking anymore or some shit? Like he thought I actually wanted this? He bought me some lingerie that I'd barely fit into when I wasn't this fat, and a vibrator. He said he was going to buy one of those real big wobbly ones, but the lady who was working recommended the small egg looking one.

So I hand the clerk my vibrator and explain my situation to him. He looks at it in the palm of his manicured hand. And then he picks it up—like a teabag, with his two polished fingernails—and drops it on the counter with this disgusted look on his face. This look like I'd just handed him my used rag. Some filthy bloody AIDS rag that I'd just shared with a hooker and homeless man and pulled out of my asshole. And he explains to me that without the packaging, without the tags, he couldn't take this merchandise back, that there is a No Return Policy on opened sex toys and undergarments.

And I tell him that I couldn't help it, that my idiot boyfriend thought he was smart and wrapped it in an electric sander box, that there was no packaging. But look—I still had the receipt. I hadn't used it. And he's all like, Well, you can try returning it back to the manufacturer as defective. And so I was all like, Well, couldn't you do that for me? Wouldn't it be easier for you? I'll take credit or an exchange, I tell him. It's not like I was trying to rip him off. It's not like I was dissatisfied with the product.

And he just shakes his head and wipes his hands with some Purell, and says he wishes there was something he could do, but that he can't—the sale is final. He only works here, he says. He doesn't make the rules.

Whatever. I was done whining and begging and grovelling. I didn't need this shit. So I was all like, Fine. Here. Take it... take it you fucking Jew. Stick it in your queer-hole for all I fucking care.

And I like throw my ginch at him and throw the egg at him and it bounces off his chest and lands like all vibrating on the counter. His reflexes are garbage and he looks all scared for his life. And I'm leaving, and I'm almost out the door, but then I change my mind and turn around and snatch my shit back, because I don't want them to have it—even if I hate it. I'd rather give it to some bum on the street. The cashier is backed up behind the counter with his hand over his throat.

And then I'm leaving for real, and I tell him that I'm going to burn the Brass Horn to the fucking ground—he'd be sorry.


## Night Market

I had the best dream last night. It was like one of those dreams that you don't ever want to end. Like one of those dreams that you become aware that you're dreaming it, and you try to chase it and hang onto it, only it's like trying to catch a dandelion or a bubble.

We were in Paris, me and my daughter. Only it wasn't really Paris, it was more like Arabian Nights Persia, and like Venice, with all the canals. It was the evening, and the city looked like one of those fancy tea tins, all blue and silver and gold. The crescent moon was big and straight out of a children's story, and I was just waiting for a cow to jump over it.

I was pushing my daughter in a Prana Sean Jean. It had like fiber optics all over it and it kept changing colors—it was beautiful. There was one of those cute little monkeys sitting on top of it, wearing a red fez and vest and smoking out of the Prana's hookah and sharing it with my baby.

My daughter was just too cute. She looked like a little doll. Like one of those sexy JonBenét babies, only smaller. She was speaking French, and I understood her—but really I don't speak French and I hate the gross accent. I was calling her Natasha for some reason. Natasha or Tasha. She'd say something adorable and I'd laugh and say, Oh Natasha, and shake my head and smile.

She and the monkey wanted some chocolate éclairs, so we had to go to the Eiffel Tower. We had to get there before it closed, to catch the elevator to the moon. And then we'd sit on the patio at the Cafe Éclair de Lune, and have coffee and éclairs and red wine and smoke long cigarettes. And we would probably like discuss philosophy and fashion and intellectual shit, but none of us would give a damn.

And we're almost there, and then the monkey starts getting all excited. Like he's all screeching and hopping up and down and doing backflips. And he snatches this ticket that's printing out of the Prana, and he waves it around and says that we won. We won the lottery. And I'm like looking at it, and it's hard to see the numbers, but all the right ones are there. And I can't believe it— he's right—we won the lottery.

And I'm like thinking, Oh my god, this must be a dream... this must be a dream. But it's not, it's like real. Like I can't wake up. And the monkey's even pinching me and I can't wake up. I'm so happy—we're rich. And now Gwyneth is pushing the Prana, only it's not really Gwyneth, she's my grown daughter. And she's pushing her baby self in the buggy and talking to me in text talk, going like, OMG, i cnt bleev we 1 th lotRE! i'm th luckiest .eR in th wrld! LOL! i <3 u so mch!!! And we're all so excited and we're going to the Parisian Night Market to shop and celebrate.

And it's like the street opens up to a valley of shops and markets and lights below, and we step onto the world's biggest escalator and go down. And the Prana and the baby don't roll down the stairs because it's not real life, it's like a perfect dream. And everything was on sale, but nobody would take our money. No, they would tell us, your money is no good here—the lottery winner gets everything for free. And we get so many spices and shoes and rare bottles of gin and wine, it's too much to carry. Only then we get this bag that looks like a Russian nesting doll. You just like put all your shit in it and fold it together and close it and everything fits. It was like magic. We must have got like hundreds of shoes and bottles and phones and spices into that Russian doll. Like all for free. It was like the best day of my life.

# New Year's

It was probably on Assbook already. Date rapes, gang-bangs, whatever—for some reason these retards think it's ok to post that shit on there. They don't realize that they could wind up sucking cock in prison for a couple months. Like negotiating for their cafeteria lunch and shit.

This idiot, I guess he's underage, had a drink and started going on about how he could drink everybody under the table. I could drink all you assholes, all you bitches under the table, he says. He's saying this shit to these douchebag looking college guys. They look like football players or some shit, and they're laughing at him. He looks twelve, like Justin Bieber with his hair, and must weigh a buck ten. He keeps whipping his head to the side to get the hair out of his eyes.

And I don't know exactly what happened. It's not like I was staring at the kid the whole time. But he got a bottle of vodka from somewhere and chugged it. It's like a big bottle, and I saw him chug over half of it. These idiots were all cheering and laughing. Some morons were smiling, looking into their phones, filming it. And about twenty minutes, half hour later, Bieber was lying on the hardwood floor, swimming in his puke.

It was huge puddle. It was fucking gross. It was like all over his clothes and all in his hair. And I saw him lift his head up, and he whipped his face to the side. Like to get the hair out of his eyes one last time, and then his face fell back in his puke. He looked dead.

So some shithead got like a broom and a towel and tried to clean up the mess. And the football players were all posing behind Bieber, like for a group photo. These retards were all going to jail if something happened to this kid. I stayed way in the background, so my face wouldn't wind up on their Assbook profiles for the cops to look at. I didn't need to be dragged into this bullshit. I crashed this party. I didn't know these people.

Finally some girl, and probably her boyfriend, grabbed the half dead kid and dragged him into the shitter. And when I walked by later, they had him in the tub. He was out cold. Four people were all around him, taking care of him. The one girl was toweling his face. And then some guy—maybe a doctor? I don't know—started smacking him and was all like, Hey... hey... can you hear me? Wake up... wake up... And then he puts his pinkies in his mouth and whistles loud into Bieber's ear, and smacks him in the face again.

All the drama made me drink faster. I still had a bottle in my bag, but I went to the kitchen to get a free one. So I poured myself another drink, and then I heard someone behind me. She's all like, Oh, hey... Bella, right? So I turn to see who it is, and I'm all like, Oh, heeey... how's it going? Like I'm excited to see her, even though I don't know who the hell she is. I'm stunned for a few seconds, and then she says that we met here before, at the costume party. Natasha. The girl with the alien. And I see her pregnant gut and I'm all like, Oh of course—ya ya, I remember you—I barely recognized you without the blood... I actually wanted to call you, but I lost your card. Wow. What are the odds? And then I lie and tell her my name is Samantha.

So Natasha looks at the counter, and at all the drinks on it, and she smiles, like she's sharing a secret with me, and is all like, Man... I cannot wait to have a glass of wine...

And I'm all like, Oh, I know, *I know*... me too! I could strangle somebody for a drink right now... oh well. And then I take a sip of my vodka and laugh at her like we're best friends.

She asks if I'm here with my boyfriend. I tell her he's already left, got called into work—it gets crazy around the ER at this time of the year. But Robert really left because this girl that Tyler was after was acting all slutty and hanging off some other dude, so Tyler got in a shitty mood and wanted to fuck off. Robert asked if he could go too, if I would mind. They wanted to go to the bar—he'd catch up with me later, he says. It was fine by me. Easier to drink when he's not around.

Natasha's at the party by herself too. Her ex lives in Australia, doesn't even know she's pregnant. It's a long story. And she doesn't really know anyone here—these are all her cousin Zoey's friends. Zoey hooked up with some guy a couple of hours ago and she hasn't seen her since. So much for taking care of her, she says. And then she's all like, Oh well, we can ring in the new year together.

And we're talking, and having a good conversation, and I'm actually starting to like this girl. It was like she was so nice, like I didn't even feel jealous of her. But god, she was beautiful, and at eight months she hardly looked it. Why the hell did I get this fat? And then the music turns down, and people start leaving, pouring out of there real quick.

I guess Bieber was getting worse. Like he stopped breathing for a minute, and somebody finally called an ambulance. You could hear a chick running around, like all shrieking, I called an ambulance! I called an ambulance! Everybody... the cops are gonna be here... this kid needs an ambulance... I called an ambulance!

So we're taking off. Natasha gives me her card again and writes her private cell number on the back, and tells me to give her a call this week. Maybe Tuesday, Wednesday? We have to go for tea, she says. I tell her for sure. And that I'll be getting a new number this week—I'll give it to her then.

You never saw people clear out of a party so fast. It wasn't even midnight yet. They were pouring out of there like some guy in a turban dropped off a suitcase. Some package with an alarm clock, wires, and AIDS that was going to blow up at midnight. The place was almost empty by the time I got out of there. And I'm not sure, but I think the kid died.


## Shocker


They really messed this one up. I mean, not completely, not entirely, but in the end it, this was just not what I expected.

It was my last day at work, and the girls threw me a big going away party. I think it was even better than Frona's. They only surprised her after work with a cake and luggage and some other travel shit and we all went out drinking. With my party, they actually decorated the office at lunch while I was out. With like baby blue and pink balloons. There was a cut-out stork and streamers and everything, it was so nice. They even closed the office for half the day, so it was like a paid staff party.

And it was a Friday afternoon, so management even bought some booze and offered cab rides home for everyone. There was beer and wine and a couple of punch bowls. One was for the drivers and the pregnant people, the other was for the drinkers. Not even Nancy noticed I was drinking from the spiked bowl.

It was a pretty laid back party, and people were doing the usual party shit. Laughing, talking shop, talking stupid shit about work, picking scraps from the meat tray like a bunch of drunk animals. Like a pack of alcoholic hyenas. Nobody was making out yet, but it was early, and most of the people I work with are fucking ugly anyways.

So after a while, Alex, one of our managers, starts clinking his glass with a knife to get everyone's attention, like he's making some kind of an announcement. He starts off with some lame joke I didn't hear or can't remember and a few people laugh. And then he's more serious, like reflective. Like about how they were sorry they didn't have the budget to throw a proper New Year's party this year. Something about the recession. Tough economic times. How it was a challenging year for Petrus Cheong and Associates Global. How we lost a lot of clients. How he hopes that this little party will show the company's and management's appreciation. And I'm ready to throw the guy a fucking violin, but then he turns the attention to me.

He says some nice things about me, which is weird,

because I don't really know him and I don't think we've ever spoken to each other. But it was kind of sweet anyways. And it probably looks like I'm blushing, like I'm embarrassed by all the attention, but it's only the booze. Then he goes on about a couple of baby pools, like a birthday pool, and another one for how much the baby is going to weigh. And now I'm really interested because they're going to give me half the money. And Alex cracks another joke, which I didn't hear because I'm still thinking about the money but laugh at anyways, and then he calls Daphne up to talk.

You can tell Daphne used to be a hottie back when she was like in her twenties. Like she was probably a slut, getting lots of abortions and shit. But now she was like forty, and married, and more of a cougar I guess. She looks like she'd cheat on her husband if she had a few drinks.

Anyways, I like Daphne as far as work people go. She's popular around the office. Her speech is funnier, like less formal than Alex's. She's getting more laughs. Saying shit like she'll hardly notice I'm gone because I'm only there maybe once a week, asking if she can bet on twins for the baby pool—I'm so fucking fat, shit like that. And then she goes on about how all I ever talk about is this Prana buggy, like I own shares in it—and then my heart stops. Seriously, I thought I was going to have a jammer. Daphne says she hopes I appreciate how hard it was to find one in guacamole, and then asks me to come over and join her.

So I go up to Daphne and she hugs me and hands me a card, and everyone's like clapping. And then Jen pushes the buggy in from the door behind us, and I see it and my jaw drops. I can tell right away that they fucked this one up.

The Prana Green Tara Serenity.

I mean, you can't call it a budget or ghetto model—it's a Prana. But seriously, I would've rather they'd gone to Wal-Mart and gotten their exclusive Prana Pink Chocolate Shocker 2P-1S. Like for cheaper even. At least I could jog with that one. This was like what an old woman would push around. Like a walker. I'd look like some fucking grandma shitting her diapers, having a stroke and hanging off her walker. Showing off her dull old baby to her dull old friends. Doing it all in slow motion.

How did this happen? Really? That... that *thing*... It's just... it's so not me. It's just so not me. This was all just so not fair.

I faked like I loved it, It's sooo nice! Oh my god! I can't wait to use it! How did you know this is what I wanted? I was hugging everybody. Oh my god you are all way too nice. I'm so sad I'll be gone for so long, I'm going to miss you all so much... But really I just want to cry. I did start crying, but it looked like happy tears. That buggy was fucking garbage. It looked garbage hell. And it's not like I'm crazy, it's not like I thought that they were trying to be nasty. I mean, everybody likes me, but fuck, they messed this one up. For real—how the hell do you get *Serenity* mixed up with *Che Revolution*?

I pulled myself some more punch. I ate a piece of cake. I ate three pieces of cake, and then I ate another before I left. It was a beautiful cake. It looked like a sleeping baby, the detail was amazing, and the actual cake was a rich red velvet torte. They had it done up at the Baker's Dozen on Kordova—which in my opinion makes the best honey glazed donuts in the city. At least they didn't fuck that up.

## OBO

FOR SALE

Prana Green Tara Serenity.
Brand new, never used.
Looks sharp. Guacamole.
No bedbugs.
Asking $600 OBO
Willing to trade/pay extra for
Prana Red Tara—Che Revolution
or similar model.
New only, please.

## Orbit Beach

Work was for suckers. For real. Once I had my baby I was seriously going to start looking at other ways to make money. My first day of freedom felt awesome. The city looked different. The people weren't as ugly. It was like being on holidays, like in some foreign country. Or at least what I imagined it would feel like to be in another country. It was like I was alive. Energized. I had all sorts of motivation. The world felt big and new. Like right after you quit school. When the possibilities are endless and it's like life is just starting. Like you have all the time in the world. It felt like I was on the verge. Like on the verge of better things, of exciting times.

I started my first day off in the park, sitting on a bench. It was a perfect winter morning. Like sunny, not too cold. Everything sparkled. I had my thermos of coffee and was enjoying a cigarette. And there was a bottle of whisky in my handbag, which I kept adding to my coffee. I brought some bread, like for the birds. I felt bad for them, with the cold and all. Seriously, I could get used to this life of leisure. I thought maybe I'd do this somewhere in the Mediterranean in a few months. But I don't know, a kid changes everything.

There was like a plaque on my bench. It was dedicated to Dr. Xiang (Ernie) Hu. I wondered if he was like a for real doctor, or maybe a master of chi doctor—like prescribed bear gall bladder and tiger penis to his patients. Maybe I'd google it if I remembered. It says he enjoyed spending weekends here with his dog, walking along the beach. And for a few seconds, I was like horribly depressed. You live your whole life, work hard, try to be a good person, create, I guess, like a legacy, all so you can... get your name put on some bench. To get shit on by birds. To get shit on by some drunken bums.

But it was a nice view, I thought. I could sit here all day and look at the water, the bridge, the skyline. And it must have been gorgeous at sunset when it was all like pink and orange. You could do worse, I guess. But whatever, I was too buzzed and medicated to get bummed out by some dumb bullshit like a bench anyways.

I saw the lighthouse out in the bay. There was like a couple of them. But the one I was looking at, I swear that when I was a kid, I walked out to it. Maybe I didn't. Maybe it was like all a dream, or I like saw it on the news, but I sort of remember it as a field trip or some shit. Some trip that my class took when I was like six or seven. The yellow school bus. My pink gum boots. The starfish and seashells.

It only happens like maybe once every year or two, when the tide is at its lowest. There's this land bridge, like a crescent, and you can walk out to the light house, like for real. Like you don't even need a boat. There's a lot of people when it happens. They start from one end of the beach, go to the lighthouse, and end up on the other end of the beach. It was on the news sometimes even.

Anyways, I was almost out of coffee, and I wasn't going to drink straight whisky this early in the morning. I figured I'd better hit up the Starbucks. But I had enough for another cup and I was close to my car, so no big deal. The Escalade was parked right behind me, through the bushes. There must have been twenty little lots like this in the park, but as far as I could tell, this was the best one. I was the only one parked here today.

The bench I sat on was at the tip of a V in the trail—like the muff of the trail. If I looked at the beach I could see anybody coming either way. On average, someone, or like people, passed by me twelve times an hour. Like once every five minutes. The shortest time between people was over twenty seconds, the longest was twelve minutes. There were five dog walkers—three couples, and two with just their dogs. There were five joggers—two groups, and three single joggers. And there were two walkers. One of them was pregnant. Six, seven months, I guessed. We smiled at each other.

I'd do this all week. Count the people. Find the best days. The best times. I poured myself the last of my coffee. I almost pulled the wrong bottle from my handbag, but then I found the whisky and gave myself a shot. I figured I'd wander around town. Maybe go shopping. Take a nap later. Whatever. I had the entire day ahead of me.


# Bamboo Ice


*Natasha St. Allegra.*
*Agent, Vivendi Nova Realty*


I had no trouble finding her card this time. God, she was photogenic. She looked like a model, a high priced escort or some shit, not like a real estate agent. I called her. She actually recognized my voice, and I blushed and I couldn't stop smiling. So we talked for a bit and decided on lunch.

We met at this place by the University, The Banyan Leaf. It's like a vegetarian restaurant, with all sorts of Buddhas and shit all over the place. There were like students and smart people, vegetarians and hippies hanging out there. Our waitress dropped off our menus. She had like messy hair and dark rimmed glasses, and you could just tell she had a big bush.

And I was looking at the menu and I really didn't know what to get. So I asked Natasha what was good. She loves it here, everything's good, she says. Was I hungry? Did I just want something with coffee or tea? Was I having any cravings?

I was starving. But I was feeling totally fat and didn't want to look like a fucking pig in front of her. Like shove a foot long veggie burrito down my throat or some shit. So I asked her what she's going to have?

She's not really hungry, she says, which sucked. She was just going to have coffee and cheesecake. She only drinks coffee every other day while she's pregnant, but the coffee and cheesecake here are probably the best in the city. Get the cheesecake, she says, any cheesecake—you'll love it, and the coffee's awesome.

So the waitress came back and took our orders, and a few minutes later she brought us our food. Natasha was right. It was probably the best cheesecake I've ever eaten, and the coffee's right up there too. I bet I could eat an entire cake it's so fucking good. So I'm all like doing one of those stupid Food Network faces, like I'm having an orgasm from sticking this shit in my mouth, and I tell her, Oh my god... Natasha, you are *so* right... this is *so fucking good.*

And then I tried to think of something to talk about. I really didn't want to start with the weather and shit because that's fucking lame and I wanted her to like me. So I tell her about my dream. I tell her about the one I had this morning. It was so weird, like the Pope became my surrogate mother, like the Vatican was changing some of its rules or shit to prove a point. It made no sense, even for a dream. And that was all I could remember about it. And I admit it—it's not a very good one. I tell her that I've got better ones.

Then I shove the last of the cheesecake into my mouth

and ask her if she's ever noticed that people always start describing their dreams by saying, *I had the weirdest dream last night,* or they'll say, *My cat does the weirdest thing* before they bore you with their shitty cat stories.

And she looked like she was kind of thinking about it for a second, and then she's all like, Hmmm, the superlatively weird preface... And then she laughs and says that no, she hadn't really noticed it before. But now that I mentioned it, ya, it was true. It's almost like a universal law, she says. And I don't know what the hell she's talking about but I'm glad that she's agreeing with me.

And then I tell her about more of my dreams—I've been having all sorts of pregnant dreams. I tell her about the one where my baby was a retard. How embarrassing it was, how horrible it was. How my baby tried to kill me and I had to drown it. What a nightmare.

She says she doesn't remember her dreams so much, but maybe I'm just nervous. Maybe I'm just a little stressed out about having a baby. That I probably shouldn't worry about it. It's only natural to be a little anxious.

And then she kind of changes the topic—asks if I'm doing ok with all the preparation and shit? Do I need anything? And I'm all like, Oh, ya ya, everything's good. And she says that if I do need anything, she knows a couple people through work. They just had kids a couple of years ago and offered her some shit they didn't need anymore.

And I'm all like, Oh, I think I'm ok... About the only thing I need is a stroller.

And then I take a sip from my empty coffee cup, and tell her, like all casual—I'm thinking about a Prana may-

be... the Prana Red Tara—Che Revolution SR... I've uh...
I've *heard it's pretty good.*

And she's all like, Oh my god—that's what I wanted to
get... Those are really the best for jogging. They have the
lowest weight to size ratio on the market. I love them.
And she goes on about the Prana Red Tara—Che Revolution SR for a few minutes. She knows more about them
than I do. And then she says that she can get me one. She
can get me one *for free.* It's used—if I don't mind used—
but her friend at work was going to give it to her. Her
friend absolutely loved that buggy, she says. Took real
good care of it. It's like new.

And I mean, I know I just met her and she's like being
an awesome friend and only trying to help—but there's
no way that I want a fucking used stroller. Something
that's been shit in. Pissed in. Sweat on. Just so gross. But
then I go to her, Like for real? Holy shit, wow... that is so
*awesome...* Thank you! That is so awesome of you! But I
mean, don't you want it? Like... for yourself?

And she's all like, Oh I would—absolutely. It's in perfect condition—I've seen it. But I don't need it. A former
client got me the Prana Bamboo Ice for Christmas...

The Prana Bamboo Ice. *Mother Bear. Ferocity in love.* It's
the stroller celebrities use. Limited edition. Fully loaded.
Expensive. All profits go to buy parcels of land in the
Chinese rainforests, and icebergs or some shit. Like to
set up sanctuaries or protected areas for the endangered
Red Panda and the Polar Bear. And the actual buggy is
completely carbon neutral. Vegan. Officially Good Karma
Certified by Tibetan monks. The frame is made from
bamboo, recycled materials, and fair trade metals from
artisanal mines in Mexico. The plastic is all from pollut-

ed beaches, and whatever can be recovered from the Great Pacific Garbage Patch.

And I can't believe that she just dropped that she's got a Bamboo Ice and isn't even bragging about it. She changes the subject even.

We ordered more cheesecake and coffee and talked for like another half hour. We talked about all sorts of shit. I told her how I didn't like it when singers laughed in songs, how it sounded fake and ugly. How I hated most drivers and have accidentally run a couple of cars off the road. How I hated the term Happy Dance. I told her all sorts of shit I didn't like. But mostly I learned a lot about her. Like I mean, I was getting to know her.

And then she had to go, get back to work. Where's the time gone? she says. I offered to pay the bill, but she insists that she's got it. Which was fine by me—I didn't want to pay that bad.

And before she leaves, I ask her, Natasha... do you have any other pregnant friends? Like, do you know other pregnant people? And she kind of looks at me like she doesn't really understand the question, and she's all like, No, not really. She says that she's not in any pregnancy groups or programs or any shit like that, if that's what I mean. Why?

And I'm all like, Oh, no reason, you've just been so helpful—it's been really nice having someone to talk to. I've just really liked hanging out with you. I don't have a lot of girlfriends anymore.

And then she's all like, No worries, it's no trouble. And she's smiling, and I think that she's had a good time, like for real. At least I hope she has. Then she says to call her again. Any time is good, but Tuesday or Wednesday would be best. She's busy with work for the next week or two, getting everything tied up and finished. And then she's going to be busy with the baby.

So then we left. She got into her VW and smiled her model smile and waved goodbye. And I wished that I'd met her sooner, that we were like old friends. That things could be different.

But whatever, I was just dying for a smoke. I didn't have one all day because I didn't want to smell like cigarettes around her. So I lit one and walked around the block. It was a beautiful day out. The sky was like silver. And I was walking and smoking and I passed by this couple. They looked ugly, sketchy. Like junkies. Fucking crackheads or some shit. And they were like holding hands. And at first, I was thinking—why even bother?

But then I kind of thought it was cute. It's like they were saying, I like you... I like you and I enjoy smoking crack with you.

## Peanut butter cups

He was all sweaty and wild eyed. Like in a panic. It was about nine in the morning—Robert just got home, and I just got up. I hadn't even grabbed a coffee yet.

He was a mess. Seriously. Like he just crawled out of the ashtray. He looked all crazy and confused and smelled like the campfire. So I was all like, Holy shit, Boo, what the hell happened? He ran his hand through his dirty hair and suddenly he looked like Buckwheat. He was out of breath, and was all like twitchy and gross, and just he kept going, I was here all night... I was here all night... If anybody asks, I was here all night...

And then he went straight to the fridge and grabbed a couple beer and took them to the shower. When he got out a few minutes later, he cracked another beer and apologized—says he ran all the way home. There was a fire, he says. A fire at the loft.

And I was all like, What!? Holy shit! Oh my god, what happened... what the hell happened? Are you ok? Is everyone ok? Tell me what happened... So he tells me the story, and I can't fucking believe it. It's just too stupid. I tell him I can't believe Dean wasn't there.

And then he looks at the ground, like embarrassed, like he's just been busted. Like the retard who just shit his pants and knows he's got to be changed. He tells me that Dean was there. It was Dean's idea, he says. He's been out of the hospital for about a month now. Was staying at Tyler's the last couple of weeks. He didn't want to tell me—said he knew that I'd get mad.

I hadn't seen Dean for weeks. I didn't want to be anywhere near that idiot during the holidays. It was awesome. But I guess the dream was over. It was like I was the moron who gets cancer all over again. And I mean, I guess—deep down—I always knew it. I knew that he'd be back. I knew he wouldn't just crawl under some rock and die. It was all too good to be true.

Robert says that Dean's lawyer settled the case with the apartment owners. He got five thousand dollars—down from the two hundred thousand his ambulance chaser was after. Dean blew it all in a couple of days. Debts, weed, gold grillz, cornrows, extensions, and a used red scooter. And then he borrowed another few hundred bucks to pimp the scooter. Boo says Dean doesn't need it—that he can walk ok. He says he waddles like there's a motion sensitive bomb up his ass, but he can walk ok. The scooter's just so he can collect disability.

And Robert's telling me this, and I'm feeling horrible, just terrible, for the poor bastard who had to fit those grillz over his busted snaggleteeth.

So Robert, Dean, Tyler, Josh, and a couple other guys I don't know, are hanging out at the loft last night. And around five a.m., Josh gets up to go to work, and gives his friends a lift home. So now Robert, Dean and Tyler are playing video games and smoking and drinking. Dean gets this idea into his ugly head that they should make peanut butter cups. There's a 7-11 a block away. And instead of buying themselves some fucking peanut butter cups, they buy some overpriced chocolate and overpriced peanut butter. It'll be fun, Dean says.

He's done this before. It's good, it's going to be so good. You just melt the chocolate in a metal bowl. You put the bowl in a pot of boiling water, and that way you can't burn it like you can in the microwave. When the chocolate's melted, you divide it into two portions, making sure they both stay warm. Then you get a muffin tin and paper muffin cups and pour half the chocolate in it. When the bottoms and sides are covered, you spoon in the peanut butter, and then pour the remaining chocolate on top. Refrigerate. Once cooled, you bang the muffin tin upside down onto a cookie sheet, and enjoy. Only they couldn't find a muffin tin, so they were going to use ice cube trays.

And I'm stunned. I don't think he even knows how to

boil water. The retard can barely use a microwave. Like for real—I actually showed him how to set it once. But suddenly it's like Dean was fucking Betty Crocker. The Kitchen Fabio. The Rachel Ray of 7-11. Like he took the Master Chef course in his spare time at the hospital. What a bunch of shitheads. They couldn't just buy peanut butter cups like a million other stoners. And I just shake my head, like I'm amazed, like I'm disgusted. Amazed and disgusted that anyone could be so stupid.

Don't worry, Dean says, I'll make them... they're gonna be so good... Reese's will taste like dogshit after you try the Weedman's...

So Dean goes to the kitchen, Tyler's crashed out in his room, and Robert's playing a racing game.

About a couple beer later, Robert smells smoke. He calls Dean, but Dean's not answering. So Robert gets up and sees Dean on the couch. His eyes and mouth are open and he's snoring. Robert can see his new grillz. Then he sees the smoke and runs to the kitchen.

I guess the Iron Chef let the pot boil dry, so the chocolate caught fire. Robert throws a beer on it, and the fire splashes all over the cupboards and spreads. And then he's all like *holy shit,* and runs to wake up Dean. He smacks him and shakes him and tells him there's a fire. He runs into Tyler's room and yells for Tyler to wake up. Tyler rolls over and tells him to fuck off. So Robert's all like, There's a fire! There's a fucking fire! Wake up! So Tyler gets up all in a tired panic and is like, *Fuck... fuck...* Josh is gonna kill us... Josh is gonna kill us... and he starts looking around for a fire extinguisher. The place is filling up with smoke real quick.

Robert and Tyler are in the kitchen trying to put the

fire out, and then Dean runs right by them. Doesn't say a word. He just runs right past the kitchen, throws open the door, and disappears. And Robert says that as soon as the door opened, the place became a fireball. There was like an instant wall of flames, and Robert and Tyler had to run through it to get out. Robert throws the fire alarm and they run down the stairs.

Dean and his scooter are gone. Tyler throws his shirt off and rolls around on the ground, and Robert's whacking him with his jacket. He's not sure how bad Tyler's burns are, but it's cold out so he tells him to keep the jacket and says that he's got to go. He's sorry and apologizes—but he's got to get the hell out of there before the cops show up.

Tyler says not to worry. Tells him to hurry, to get out of there. He's like coughing and shaking, sitting on the curb. And then Robert hears the sirens coming, and he runs. He says that he ran for like an hour, didn't stop once, until he finally got home.

Robert's exhausted. Overtired. Paranoid. He's sure it's the end of the world. He's violated the terms of his probation. The cops are going to knock on the door any minute. He's going to get dragged out and thrown in jail for sure. And he keeps whining, mumbling, going on and on, and I finally notice that his eyebrows have been burned off and he looks like he's gotten way too much sun.

I'm getting bored listening to his shit, so I cut him off—I tell him not to worry about it. He didn't light the damn fire. If anyone was going to catch shit, it was going to be Dean. And I tell him that he's a hero. He pulled the fire alarm. He saved Tyler. He should be proud of himself. The cops will look shitty arresting a hero. And I tell him not to worry—they'll probably never even know he was there.

Only he doesn't hear any of it. He's already crashed out on the couch with his open beer.


# Mitchell Island


I was sitting on the park bench, staring at them like a retard for I don't know how long. Like they were a herd of unicorns or some shit. Like I was a lost unicorn and would be reunited with them soon. They were exercising with their babies. Most of them were in really good shape. I was going to have to lose a lot of weight before I started any sessions with them. Whatever, I had plenty of time to stop eating.

Boo fucked off to Mitchell Island. It was for the best, really. The guy's been a complete mess the last few days. A total disaster. Drinking all the time, paranoid about the cops, peeking out the windows, jumping and hiding around corners whenever the phone rang. Like John Walsh or *To Catch a Dirty Pedophile* Chris Hansen were out to get him.

He joked with me before he left, said to wait to have the baby until he got back. Stick a cork in it. He hated to be away when the baby was born, but he said he'd rather lay low at his family's place than wreck his asshole in prison. He gave me his new number—he lost his old phone in the fire. I tried it, but the voice mail wasn't set up yet.

I drank the last of the hot buttered rum from my

thermos. And then I got like this déjà vu or some shit of being lost and drinking Patrón in Vegas. I wasn't sure why, but whatever. The mothers were all leaving. They were all smiling, laughing, saying bye to each other. It was beautiful out, but cold. I figured I might go watch *Breaking Dawn* again this afternoon. Catch a matinée. I don't know why those guys fuss over that little bitch.

I walked to the public shitters and found a payphone that worked. Natasha sounded like she was happy to hear from me. Like for real happy, like she wasn't even faking it.


## Venus


She had no idea that I wanted a new place, and I mean really, neither did I. But she was more than happy to help. Of course she would show me around. She's got a perfect listing for me. I was going to love it. It was about an hour out of town. A great place to start a family, to raise a kid, but still close enough to the city to commute.

I was late. I was halfway up the path and Natasha had the door open and was all like waving at me. And I was starting to say sorry but she's all like, Come in, come in! Hurry! It's freezing out! So I followed her inside and she's hugging and rubbing her arms like she's cold, and then she sort of laughs and says that maybe she shouldn't have invited me in. And then I get this jolt of panic like I've never felt in my life. Like a headrush and my heart stops and I can't see. And then she's all like, You're not supposed to invite vampires into your home, right Bella?

And then I get it and probably laugh a little too much. And she smiles and apologizes for her dumb joke, but it's crazy how much I look like Bella from the side she says. And so I'm all like, Ya, No... You don't have to worry about me... I'm just a girl.

And then she asks if I made it here ok. Was it snowing anywhere yet? She heard it was supposed to start snowing today or tomorrow. And I apologize again because I'm like twenty minutes late. Traffic was shit through the city and I got a little lost once I was in the neighborhood. And then she tells me no worries—she didn't mean it like that, and that she tried calling me, but she must have gotten my new number wrong. It kept saying it wasn't in service.

And I'm all like, Oh that is just so weird—I've had that happen to me all week. And I shake my head like I'm sad, frustrated, disgusted. Like I've just had enough. Like I've just been strip searched and cavity searched in front of everybody at the airport for no good reason. And I go on about how I've been kept on hold with these phone company shitheads for hours, how they still can't figure out why my account keeps getting deactivated. I've only been with these animals for like two weeks, and I already want to cancel.

So Natasha's nodding, like she's all sympathetic, like she's going *I know, I know, me too, me too.* And then she says that she feels horrible—that she tried getting a hold of me—but would I mind it so much if we had lunch tomorrow? She has to show this place again in a half hour. She feels sick about it.

And I can tell she feels bad. She really wanted us to

check out this gastrolounge, Ice³, on the way back into town. Like to eat, not to drink. It's getting great reviews. A real modern dining experience. The tapas is supposed to be just awesome. Real sophisticated.

And she explains that this married couple who were supposed look at the place yesterday had an emergency and asked if they could reschedule for today. But she tells me not to worry about it. That if I want the place, it's mine. Just a formality unless I don't want it.

No worries, I tell her. We can go anytime, I understand.

Then she cheers right up, and tells me to follow her—she'll show me around.

So she starts showing me around, and it's not like I'd know, but she's really good at her job. She knows everything about the house. The granite countertops, the double wall oven, the geothermal heating and the types of flooring in every room. There's like a school just a few blocks away that consistently ranks in some top ten. How she figures the house would qualify for some LEED certified bullshit.

And she doesn't want to pressure me in any way, but she says that really—now is the best time to buy a house. The market hasn't recovered yet. The owner's a distressed seller. The interest rates have never been this low. Everything's lined up in my favor. Like it's in the stars, like some magic window's been opened. In ten years, if I want to sell, I'll be very happy. Sometimes, Natasha tells me, we have to take advantage of opportunities like this. We have to take advantage before they slip away. Then she wants to show me the wood stove, how perfect it is on a day like today.

So I'm following her, but I feel like we're being led along some track. Like we're being carried on karmic wheels, on cosmic gears. And she keeps talking but I can't understand what the hell she's saying anymore. My head's in a different place. It's like I'm floating, watching everything from outside of my body, like an air Shiva or air Kali or some shit. Like I'm on some primordial plain. Time is gone. And I'm living in the moment.

I grab something off a side table. I recognize it. It's one of those Venus figurines. Like a fertility statue of some pregnant bitch—or it could just be a fat chick. I don't know, there's like different theories about their purpose, their meaning. The real ones are some of the oldest art in the world. They're a bit of a mystery, really. But whatever—it'll do.

Natasha's guiding me, walking in front of me. And I mean, I'm not totally sure, but I think that this is going to be ironic for one of us.


## Keys to happiness


She's fine, she's ok—she's just a little sick... she has violently explosive diarrhea... we're lesbians... we're trying to have sex... can you please just leave us the fuck alone?

I didn't know what the hell to say. I just wanted to tell him to fuck off, but the best I come up with is Hi. And the kid's just standing there like a retard, straddling his dirt bike and staring at us with his squinty rat eyes. I was parked by the river on the dirt road, standing by the open back door, and Natasha's legs were hanging out. I guess it did look kind of weird.

But for real, what the fuck was he doing riding his dirt bike around in the freezing cold for anyways? No helmet. Just a scarf and a wool cap. And he didn't say anything, he just kept looking at us, with his dumb red face. I hoped he'd get frostbite.

So I was all like, Cold out, isn't it? And I smiled. Then he kind of grunted and kick started his bike and took off up the road. And when I couldn't hear him anymore, I pulled Natasha off the back seat. She looked like Snow White or Sleeping Beauty or some shit. Like some dead Eastern European prostitute. But she was still alive. And I didn't want her getting up, so I shoved another rag full of halothane into her face. Her beautiful bitch face.

And I was having a real shitty go. It was hard pulling her across the rocks, across the dirt. Dragging her by the hair across hardwood flooring was easy compared to this. But eventually I got her to the river, to this spot where nobody could see us, where nobody could hear us. And I had my clean towels and my gloves and my shit all ready, but then I couldn't find the boxcutter.

I looked everywhere for it. Behind the seats, on the floor, under the seats. I checked all my pockets. Nothing. And then I looked in my handbag. A bottle of halothane, a mickey of vodka—both plastic. Cigarettes. Toilet Paper. An egg that I forgot was in there and didn't want to break—the face looked so real. All useless. And then I looked at my keys.

And I admit it—it was messy. It was gross. There was like blood everywhere. Like a lot of blood. Natasha really wasn't looking alive. And if she was still breathing, it was just barely. But it really didn't matter anyways—I wasn't going to drive her to the hospital. I mean, I'd thought about it, but I couldn't. She almost knew who I was. So I dragged her across the rocks and the sand, over to the river.

The surface was mostly frozen, and I pushed her halfway into this hole. The water pulled her the rest of the way under. It was so quiet. Maybe she'd float away—drift off and become frozen in the ice somewhere—and they'd find her a hundred years later.

I rinsed myself off a bit. The water was fucking freezing, like my hands were going to fall off with frostbite or some shit. Then I grabbed her handbag, her phone, the duct tape and anything else I could think of, and threw it all in the river. I took off my bloody afterbirth sweater and pants and threw them in the river too.

I got back to the Escalade real quick to heat it up, it was so fucking cold out. And I was about to stick the key into the ignition but I noticed the blood on it. So I wiped it off and stuck the bloody asswipe under a rock. I wasn't going to get that shit in my car. Then I threw on my yoga pants and hoodie as fast as I could and checked the baby. She was still alive. And I mean—I'm no doctor—but premature kids are born in ditches all over the world, and I thought she was looking pretty good, and that I did ok with the bellybutton.

I wrapped her up all snug and tight. I just wanted to keep looking at her—she looked just like me—but I knew we had to leave fast. Leave before it started snowing. Leave before that retard got back. Leave before anybody found us.

A few minutes later we got off the gravel and onto the pavement. The smooth road made me feel a lot better. I sucked back probably half a mickey of Grey Goose and popped a couple of pills—I don't even know which, I just found them in my hoodie. The first flakes of snow started drifting across the windshield, and the sky was getting darker. For real, it was all pretty good timing.


## Shampoo


She was quiet when I let her out of the suitcase. I was almost scared she was dead, but she wasn't.

I got her cleaned up and settled into the motel room with her. We would spend the night, out of the freezing cold. I wasn't sure about tomorrow, or the day after that. I hadn't figured everything out yet, but I wasn't worried. I'd figure it all out later, like I always do. Right now the plan was to drink my vodka, to calm down, to go to sleep. I had a couple of bottles ready, and a thimble for her too, if she started crying.

But she was so quiet, she never cried once. She was a good baby. So tiny. I had to keep her warm. I held her between my tits. She smelled so clean. Like strawberries. Like the strawberry shampoo I used to bathe her in the sink to get the blood and placenta and cunt from that witch off her. My clean baby. My angel. My gift from the universe.

And I would protect her. No one was going to take her from me. Ever. I mean, I wasn't worried about it, but if I had to—if the cops found me, if they knocked on that door and had us surrounded—they wouldn't get us alive. It's like, I don't know quit, I don't—but I swear to god—I would drink the rest of that fucking shampoo and lie down on top of my sweet baby if I had to. They would never take her from me.

But I wasn't worried about that. I just couldn't stop smiling at my baby. And I thought of Oprah again. My first liberator. My inspiration. And I thought of her farewell show. I've seen it like a hundred times—I cry every time I watch it. I have her goodbye speech almost memorized. And now I was like seriously thinking about naming this little angel after her. Pharo.

So many things that she said, in so many ways, validated everything I'd done. Oprah said there was a difference between thinking you deserve happiness and knowing you're worthy of happiness. And with all my hard work, all the preparation—the joy—that I'd put into this—I knew I deserved it.

This is what she encouraged all of us to do—to follow our hearts, to listen to those whispers that tell us when something isn't right, when we're not doing what we should be doing. When we're not where we should be in our lives. It is god revealing itself. Setting us on our true path. Helping us find our spark, so that we can illuminate the world. To be a beacon in our own way.

And she said that there are no coincidences, only the manifestation of the grace of god. The divine order. And that she had no regrets. And really, neither did I.

Then she shared her final thoughts—that we had been her safe harbor for the last twenty-five years, and now she hoped that we would be a safe harbor for somebody else. To love somebody. To like, make a difference in their lives.

I was going to be my angel's safe harbor. I was excited

about the future. I was going wake up every morning, thinking, How can I be an awesome mother today? How can I make my baby's day better? I felt like we were on the verge of happiness. Like I finally caught up to that silver lining on the horizon and was looking over it. Things were looking good. The fun we were going to have, Me, Baby, and Boo.

ps

Hey,

I'm going to be gone a while longer. My family won't let me go back, on account of my warrant. I haven't told them about the baby yet, it's just too complicated right now. I'm still looking for work. I'll send some money when I can.

—Robert

ps—Don't change your contact information.

9 780988 051515